Magona's Rise

Book 1

By Lucas Brady

Hardcover: 979-8-9867076-1-7
Paperback: 979-8-9867076-0-0

First hardcover edition July 2022

Written by Lucas Brady
Edited by Lucas Brady
Cover photography Copyright © 2022 Lucas Brady

Printed by KDP Print in the USA

Kindle Direct Publishing
410 Terry Ave N
Seattle, WA 98109

This book is dedicated to Kevin Sparks

TABLE OF CONTENTS

~The Beginning~

At the beginning of time, seven ancient Gods were born together to create life as we know it. The first to awaken, named The Angelic, created the Big Bang. The second, The Star, made the stars that shine brightly on the universe. The third, Death, created complex life to flourish on their inhabited planets. The fourth, The Crusher, developed feelings for the life that Death created. The fifth, The Dog, helped raise the animals among the humans. The sixth, The TV, started human life and was the researcher. He would test and record any data he could on how humans functioned. During one of his studies on the planet Inaz, he found out that a certain amount of uranium in the bloodstream could change the DNA of the creature. He feared it could be used by the wrong hands and swore to not let anyone find out.

The final, The Seventh, did not make anything. Instead, he lived on the first created planet, which he named Roan. For millions of years, the Gods lived together and oversaw the universe. They let the flow of time continue on its course, although it would not be like this for much longer. Behind the scenes, one of the Gods grew jealous of the others and wanted to be the most powerful.

The Star had been developing an undisclosed plan after spying on The TV. He learned about the tests and thought that The TV was planning to grow an army. So in 1999, The Star and The Dog banded together, left the group, and arrived on the closest planet, Earth. After The TV vaguely heard of their plans from Death, he mysteriously abandoned Roan to search for The Star and to bring him back. By the year 2000, The TV still could not track down The Star and went MIA.

Meanwhile, on Roan, The Seventh also mysteriously disappeared. Before he vanished, he would explain how he believed The Angelic was plotting something. The rest of the Gods did not believe his cries; he went crazy, trashing most of the planet and calling the place "The Doom Land." The Angelic also went missing shortly after, but his disappearance is known. He was the most power-hungry and created sentient beings to house each planet, hoping they would push away all living creatures until they had nowhere but Roan to go. According to The Seventh, The Angelic wanted to enslave all life, although midway through his plan, The Angelic's creations failed, and his body was destroyed.

The Angelic's soul and energy were transferred to the Plane of Celestial, a space between all living matter in which souls can peacefully exist. He could still interfere with the living world, but only with his thoughts. He created a tomb somewhere in the universe that, when discovered, would birth Gwyn, a mighty demiGod. Gwyn would have the power to awaken the body of Magona, and The Angelic would be born once more to enslave the galaxy.

The rest of the Gods stayed on Roan, but the once busy world of the Gods eventually turned into a death-filled, purple desert hell. As Roan crumbled into a shell of its former glory, The TV sent personal creations across the universe to find a savior.

And that's only the beginning.

~The Prologue~

The cold breeze runs through my brown combed-back hair. My breath fogs up my glasses since my mouth is covered with a fuzzy, green, and yellow scarf. The colors of said scarf do not match the rest of my outfit. Which is a nice brick-red beanie, a puffy gray jacket, black jeans, and heavy black boots. The wind continues to weave through the air, as does my beard, which is oddly lighter than my hair. Usually, my eyes are green, but as I look in my car's rear view mirror, I notice they have a blue tint.

I had just arrived at Austin's Grub, a half gas station and a half grocery store a few miles away from the East Usnax border. The large, rectangular building is decorated with colors akin to a child's art project. In the foreground of the property are two gas pumps, with only one car parked in front. After I park at the other pump, I open my blood-red flat convertible's door, and as I step out, a man approaches me from the other pump. I examine his outfit, seeing dirt-covered overalls and muddy boots. He has no shirt on, and his skin is a noticeable purple. His left hand is wrapped in some bandage, with a small area of blood dripping from the edge.

"Hello?" I ask, but no response is given. He continues to walk toward me, slowly starting to limp. I open the back door to my car without taking my eyes off him and reach for my loaded handgun. Once my fingers find the handle, I pull it out and aim it straight toward the man.

"Please help me," the man stutters. "He looks just like I do. Please save me."

"I am going to ask you to step away from me. Do not come any closer."

The man stops, which causes him to fall to the ground, onto his knees. He begins to break down, and tears stroll down his purple cheeks as the door to the other car slowly creaks open.

I keep my gun aimed at the purple man, but my eyes move to the door. I see a foot slam onto the ground from underneath the door. It looks like the purple man's boots but mudless.

"Who is that?" I boom at the purple man.

"He's an imposter," he cries out.

"The fuck does that mean?" I whisper to myself. A hand slowly grabs the door's edge, pushing it forward, revealing a man that looks identical to the purple man. The same boots and overalls, although not covered with grime, and his skin lacks the purple undertone, looking somewhat damaged. "You think this is a funny prank?"

"It's not a prank," the purple man cries out as the twin walks towards us, dragging a long rusty, blood-stained chain behind him. His jaw is open to an inhuman amount, and his tongue slithers around his mouth. Saliva drips down from the chipped lips.

"State your business," I yell, aiming my gun at the twin. His eyes dart toward me, but he continues to move toward the purple man. I take a shot at his left leg, which blasts the knee cap off like a bullet through butter. Instead of blood, an odd, thick, glowing yellow substance melts from the wound. Then, as it touches the overalls, it begins melting the fabric. Finally, the twin throws the chain at the purple man, which automatically wraps him up.

"HELP ME," he yells out. The twin pulls the chain, launching the purple man into the other's bony fingers. He latches his hand onto the purple man's throat, and I take another shot, this time in the twin's nose. The yellow goo from before pours down the nose, burning the jaw, and falling onto the pavement in a gross splat. The twin crushes the purple man's throat, spraying sparkling red blood onto the twin's face, which begins to drip down. I watch in horror as the blood builds into a long, rope-like shape, latching onto the jaw and pulling it back up.

The twin drops the decapitated body onto the ground, and all the blood crawls across the floor, latching onto the twin. Then, he pushes the jaw into place, and his skin begins to twist itself back into place. I stand in shock at what I just saw, and as I finally blink and snap back into reality, the twin, the car, everything is gone. No evidence of what had just happened remains.

I slowly open the door to Austin's Grub, which rings a bell and makes me jump. Besides the lone employee sleeping at the front counter, the entire store is empty. Next to the door is a magazine rack, and the first cover I see has some blond white woman with three tits, along with the headline: Is three better than one? The store is like a grocery store, with its aisles and aisles of food, but it is still smaller than most. There's nothing but food sold here, no cleaning products, lottery tickets, or anything else. All the lights emit a soft white glow, except for one in the back, which is flickering and sometimes turning yellow. I approach the counter, and the man jumps awake. His orange and blue striped onesie is the company-issued outfit, but nobody wears it while they work here except for this man.

"I need a fill-up on pump three," my deep voice commands the worker.

"That will be twenty dollars," the worker says as he walks to the register and waits for my money.

"Twenty? What kind of jackass do you think I am? The signs outside said two-fifty a gallon. I only need five gallons. That's..." I say as I start counting on my fingers. "...only twelve fifty. Not twenty."

The worker stares at me with an expression that perfectly pisses me off. I aggressively pull my wallet out of my pocket and pull out a crumpled ten, two ones, and two shiny quarters. Then, I slam them onto the counter, and as I storm out, I grab a magazine and pretend to accidentally throw the rack over. Then, I walk towards my car and look at the other pump. Still nothing. I throw myself into the driver's seat and stick the key in, but I don't turn the ignition on. So I open the magazine and start reading the major headlines.

Reports of uranium being stolen from secure bases all across the nation! Mad cow disease; should we be scared? Army soldiers find twins of themselves after coming back from war.

That last headline struck me.

That sounded just like the purple man's situation.

I look out the window and notice the twin holding his chain through the glass doors of Austin's Grub. I quickly turn on the ignition, and as I look out of the front window, a hand grabs the hood from out of view. I slowly roll down the window, peeking my head out, and I see a head staring at me from under the car. I jump back into my seat and slam onto the gas pedal, launching through some grass onto the long road of Route 831 towards Usnax.

As the car speeds up, the hand remains on the hood. I see the knuckles start to pulse, almost as if it was pulling something up, and pulling something up is precisely what it's doing. A body flings onto the hood, blocking my view, but letting me see who it is.

That's…me?

The body is me, with my same outfit, except covered in dirt, mud, and oil. Its body is covered in scars that leak out the same yellow sludge as the other twin. I look out the passenger side window at the passing desert to tell how close to Usnax I am. Near the border, there's a giant steel burger sign that marks one mile to Usnax, and I need to get past it. I take my foot off the pedal, squint my eyes, and then slam back onto it, and the body rolls off the window and off the car. I see it move onto the road, exploding into little chunks of yellow through my rear view mirror.

Suddenly, a ringing fills my ears. I think of any dark reason until I realize it's just my silver flip phone. I pull it out while trying to stay in the right lane. I glance at the screen and see the name Harvey flashing in all capital letters. Then, I press the answer button and set the phone on the dashboard.

"Hello?" I ask.

"Yo. I'm at the gym, and something is a bit suspicious. There are some guys in suits walking down to the basement."

"Guys in suits? Why are you at the gym? You never go on weekends. And why did you need to call me?"

"It's National Arm Day, man. Gotta beef up my arms. And you ARE part of the National Guard, so I think you have some black ops training or whatever. Anyways, they keep coming in through the back entrance holding these weird silver capsules. There are a few on the top floor. Everyone's checking them out."

"Don't engage them AT ALL. Feed me information as you watch from afar. Don't do anything stupid; I'm coming back to town for something else. I'll come right to you."

"Hold on, I'm going to check." I open my mouth to argue with him but stop myself before I do. The sound of my car's engine is all I can hear until Harvey's voice comes back.

"Yeah, I found the things, and there's a switch on one of them. They are like air canisters, the ones you'd see on divers."

"Just wait until I get there."

"I hear something coming from the canisters, it sounds like my name."

"Harvey, don't do a Goddamn thi-," I get cut off as the sound of an explosion blasts through the air. A shock wave blows into my car, denting the side and sending me flipping into the coarse sand. I slowly open my eyes as I find myself dangling upside down. A cactus is smashed through the front windshield, and parts of it are poking my right leg. I wipe my face off, and shards of glass cut my fingers as I do so. I try to breathe, but my throat is too dry to get oxygen down. I raise my arms to unbuckle, and after I do, my body slams onto the car roof and into the cactus.

My mouth lets out a loud but raspy scream as I punch through the side window, which cuts my right hand up. I pull myself out of the car and crawl along the sand as it burns my skin. I thought it was cold out today. Why is the sand warm? A breeze runs through my hair again, but the coldness leaves, and the wind turns warm. I feel my scalp grow hotter as my hair and beard start to burn straight down to the skin. Once I'm entirely onto the scolding sand, I turn my dry head towards Usnax and watch as a mushroom cloud fills the sky, and the buildings collapse and crumble to the ground. My eyes begin to close as the heat becomes too much. The sound of a distant truck opens them back up, and I turn in the opposite direction and see a large semi-truck park on the side of the road next to me. A large, burly, bearded man wearing a greasy white tank top, navy blue jeans, muddy boots, and an Austin's Grub hat runs over to my parched body.

"Hey buddy, I'm here to help you. I saw your car flip from yonder. What the hell happened over there?" he says, picking me up and laying me on the passenger seat of his truck. "Name's Terris, by the way."

"We…need to get out of here," I whisper as Terris starts to drive into the city. I try to signal him to stop, but my body won't let me. My eyes almost entirely close, but I can still see a small amount as Terris drives into Usnax.

People burning to ash and women running while holding their children are all I can focus on. The roads are covered in cracks that leak dark green liquids, most likely sewer water. The scent of smoke and feces fills my nose, but I have no power to stop smelling. Buildings begin to crack and fall all around me, and only the sounds of screaming are left in my ears. I can't even see what Terris is doing. My eyes are just trained on the outside and the horror of what's happening. I see every day innocent people starting to burst into flames, drown in the water on the side of the road, or just crumble into gray ash.

I feel the truck stop, and Terris opens the door and walks out. I raise my eyes slowly, and they are greeted by the destruction of the gym. It's completely gone, excluding one lone wall. The silhouettes of people are marked on the walls with splatters of ash forming body-like shapes.

It's just like their final moments will be remembered by a painting of burnt bodies in the shape of the screaming.

In the corner of my eye, I see Terris climb up the wreckage into the gym as a slight shock wave ripples through the air. The glass of the windows shatter, cutting more of my face, and slashing straight through my left eye. I open my right to see Terris reacting to something. He flails his arms around as his veins pop all over his body, and his skin turns green. His eyes fill with a cloud of black smoke, and they expand into large, oval-shaped black holes in his now green face. A bullet grazes his left foot from nowhere, causing him to fall and crash into the gray ground.

My body falls to the right as someone opens the truck door. All I can see are two figures carrying me out onto a stretcher. I can see white uniforms but nothing else. In the background, I notice Terris making an unworldly noise as he is wrestled to the ground by other people in uniforms. He struggles to fight back as he is tazed and whipped with a rusty chain. My vision starts to clear, and I recognize the man with the chain. He is the twin from earlier. He turns his head and winks at me before going back and whipping Terris to the ground. I'm loaded into the back of some sort of ambulance, with loads of medical equipment lining the walls and roof. The two men close the doors to the back, which have two large windows on either side.

As the car starts to drive away, I watch as, from the dirt, arms burst out and begin to pull the guards underground. Like zombies, people rise, and flashes of color strobe through the windows. Then, past the crowd, I spot someone that looks like Harvey pulling his mouth open wide and swallowing a man whole. One of the men from before walks over from the passenger seat, grabbing a needle from one of the drawers. I try to call for him, but nothing comes from my voice. He turns around, and I see an ugly, distorted face missing both of his eyes. His uniform is white like I saw before, but this time I noticed a small star on the left breast spot. He flicks the tip of the needle, which holds a dark yellow liquid. It's unlike the liquid from the twin since that one was light yellow and sludgy. This new liquid is dark yellow and more like water. The man sticks the needle into an IV pump he picks up from the ground.

"Nighty night," he says as he slams the IV needle into my right arm, and the yellow liquid flows into my veins. I feel my throat fill up and start choking on something. I lose control of my body as it shakes around. My eyelids pulse open and close, and my brain feels like it has disappeared from my body. Suddenly, everything goes dark, and I feel the air around me freeze, almost like I have been dropped into a cold sea.

I have a dream about a building collapsing as the Earth is destroyed. I don't overthink it—just a dream.

~The Rebirth~

For all my life, the harsh desert was the only thing I could see looking out my bedroom window, no matter where I lived. At home with my parents, in my janky apartment building, and even at the school I went to. I used to watch action movies as a kid, and seeing the crazy places they went would always fill my imagination with crazy scenarios. I would become disappointed the moment I remembered where I lived. Usnax was not for children. It was not for the creative, a city that breathed but never lived. The tall skyscrapers blocked the sun, which was nice since the temperature was rarely cold but didn't help the feeling of isolation. Even thirty-six years after the Usnax Bombing, which is what the survivors called it, I still watch the desert pass by the window.

I was forcefully inserted into a team of fellow National Guards that have been tasked with the mission of slaughtering any "hero" that we come across. Intel from up above describes these "heroes" as any folk that possess any otherworldly power. We here on the team describe them as comic-book characters gone wrong. None of us wanted to be on this team. Everyone I've worked with was taken from Usnax and nursed back to health, just as I was. My first team lasted me almost thirty years, but we had a run-in with a man who was able to shoot pool lane lines out of his arms. He killed my entire team but left me wounded by grinding my legs up until the skin and muscle were inside my bones. Hours after he got away, I was found by another team who were on patrol, and I have been with them until now. My legs have since been repaired, and the mess of dismembered skin lies in titanium leg-like shells.

Our group name is the Valley Forge Force, which comes from the name of the largest aircraft carrier annihilated by the mushroom cloud. When I first heard the story, I thought it was bad luck, almost like the story behind the name would happen to us somehow. But for six years, I have been proven wrong. My fellow peers consist of four other kidnapped guards and one commanding officer that guides us through our objectives. The person that spotted me halfway to hell six years ago was Shawn Jr. The other guys call him Kitty Hawk since that was the fighter jet he crashed in and was taken from in 2000. He's a man in his fifties, with a shaved head, striking yellow eyes, a large build, and has scars scratched into his skin. The next man was Mac Marvin, codenamed Dream Mountain. Shawn told me Mac was a modern hippie who loved listening to 70s music. He has long, dry strands of hair that compliment his chapped lips and baggy eyes. He never blinks, nor does he ever get sick. His skin is an unhealthy shade of green, and he reeks of fish.

Thirdly, Rink McNatalie is the most mysterious of the group. His nickname is Fetal Man, and while it has never been explained, I don't think I'm missing out on anything. Rink's hair is an interesting case. A fluff of hair that waves up sits on the tip of his head, but he has long, curly strands that flow down the sides of his face. He wears women's glasses with a milky white frame and large, circular lenses. His eyes are multicolored, with his left being blue while the right is brown. He has a cleanly shaved face, with his chin almost nonexistent. His chest is large and muscular, but he has skinny legs that make skinny jeans look loose on him. Lastly, The Right Hand Man is the leader of our small group. He cannot command us at all, but he can give us orders. Like Shawn, he has a shaved head, but his face is clean and rigid. His jawline looks like it could cut straight through a diamond. His eyes are a rainbow of colors, depending on his mood. The Right Hand Man is very secretive. He's never told us his name, where he's from, or if he's one of the yellow goo people. Which is who we have to look out for.

As I have stated before, our mission is to eliminate any "hero" we find. But the asterisk in our head is to look out for Twins. They are like the one I saw at Austin's Grub, duplicating people's looks and bleeding yellow. We've run into a few, and from what I've observed, they only copy people of power. I have seen a twin copy of someone from every US army, and some were even close friends. Although I've trusted everyone on this team for the six years I've been with them, I've been suspicious of Chuck Charles for the past three months.

Chuck Charles is the prominent leader of the Valley Forge Force. He has a gray mullet with streaks of red throughout, a wrinkly neck, and a faded tattoo of an underwater clown holding cotton candy. The color of his eyes has always been dark green, but he insists that his eyes used to be pink when he was a child. Chuck's an all-around nice guy, but he started to act strange a few months ago. We were at a labor camp searching for The Donut Master, who can create killer donut minions only from the remains of starved corpses. The base was not that big but had insulated guard tents and brick towers outlining an open area that housed famished men and children of various ages and races chained by their ankles. They were all in ghostly sync, slashing away at tomato plants and growing corn. Our group always stayed together since we were more significant in numbers, but Chuck oddly went missing while searching the guard tents. I was the only one that noticed, but he wandered back to us shortly after.

We continued with the mission, shot Donut Master with a rocket launcher, and continued to the next task. Even though Chuck started acting weirdly, nobody else realized. He wouldn't talk as much, wouldn't join us in our missions anymore, and began asking to bring back the corpses. After a while, I got used to it. But I'm still holding my suspicions.

The current mission we have is to kill The Bleeder. He was spotted last at 1933 Evesham St., West Usnax. Ironically, that's right down the street from my first apartment. As usual, we loaded ourselves with gear; riot shields, heavy assault weapons, and bulletproof helmets. They are all painted with vantablack and made of the toughest graphene. The only outfits we wear casually anymore are black Christmas sweaters, black jeans, and black tactical boots. So goes well with the dark shadows we live in.

We're all loaded into a pizza truck with a large label on the side reading Ronnie's Pizza Parlor next to an image of some sort of red cartoon bunny holding a melting slice of pizza. Chuck parks the truck in an alley between the two-story Victorian-style house and the Forbidden Fun storage warehouse. I lift the truck's back door and jump onto the wet pavement. Bricks and exposed wires cover the wall on my right and the beautiful architecture of the house on my left. A light blue house with dark brown wood outlines the corners and edges. The windows are closed with chipped white shutters slowly moving in the wind. A large chimney erupts from the house's far back side, and the smoke sign proves to me that the house is occupied.

"You know what to do now. Find him, kill him, return the body to me," Chuck says from the driver's seat. I take note of his avoidance of eye contact.

"What are you gonna do then?" Mac asks.

"I'll be here, like always," says Chuck as he rolls up his window.

"Ok, team, let's go," The Right Hand Man commands as we make our way into the backyard. It's surrounded by a short metal fence, but we can quickly jump over it. I equip my newly acquired 1911 as we approach the backdoor. We pass lawn decorations like pink flamingos, nerdy lawn gnomes, and a leaf-filled pool. From the corner of my eye, I see Mac pick up a nude gnome with sunglasses and put it in a satchel he has around his waist. We make it to the back door entrance, and The Right Hand Man signals us to be quiet. We all lower our breathing until the only noise is the sound of chirping birds and the occasional crash from a distance. I look at Mac, then at Shawn, and we all nod. The Right Hand Man readies his lever-action shotgun and places a hand on the dirty doorknob on the white and blue striped door.

He slowly turns it and applies slight pressure to the middle of the door with his shoulder. As the door opens to the inside, the smell of rot and mold fills my nose. The house is dark, but the light shining from behind lets us see a small area in front of us. I see the edge of a round table peek out from the darkness, and under it lies a polar bear fur carpet. I pull a flashlight from my back left pocket and click it on. The light illuminates the room, and we all make our way inside. Bookshelves full of books, movies, and trinkets line the right wall, while the other blue-colored walls are covered in explicit paintings and closed windows. Around the glass table sit two large, blue couches decorated with pillows of famous French paintings, along with a curved, fifty-five-inch TV mounted atop a stubby coffee table. Mac finds the remote and turns the TV on, which displays a movie. While nobody can tell which movie it is, it comes right to my mind.

The movie is Wrench, a 1995 movie starring Sacul Bradley and Venus Plaque, not that it's crucial. After Mac starts to watch the film, Shawn taps him on the back and gives him a disappointing look. Rink and The Right-Hand Man walk into the next room, which has a long staircase leading to darkness, a coat stand with a ripped purple fedora, and a locked metal door. The wallpaper is instantly disgusting as it is blue, like the other room, but covered in human excrements.

"Who's going upstairs?" I ask. Everyone exchanges glances, but nobody volunteers. "Fine. Mac, you come with me."

I point at Mac, who groans but starts to follow me up the stairs. The creaking of the poorly painted white wooden stairs makes sneaking worthless, and the railing feels like it will fall at any moment. The roof begins to slope inward as the darkness grows around me, and I begin to feel watched. I turn around to talk to Mac, but he's gone. I swallow my worries and continue through the darkness, with only a flashlight to give me light. As the stairs level into the floor, I feel a cold wind flow from every direction. I hold my pistol out in front of me, with the flashlight under it, when I feel something cold drip onto my hand. I look up to see a mutilated corpse hanging from the ceiling with a rope around its neck. I let out a scream, then a knocking sound echoes from beyond the darkness. I frantically thrash my flashlight around, illuminating the space around me. I can't see anything but dusty walls with torn wallpaper, molding doors lining the hallway, and a broken cabinet on the opposite wall from where I'm standing.

The knocking sound echoes once more, and I realize the sound is coming from the cabinet. I slowly approach the cracked, torn cabinet with etchings of mice crawling up the edges. The double doors start to creak as I get ever so closer. The noise begins to sound like my name, almost as if the cabinet is beckoning me to open it. I reach out, open the left door, and shine my light in. I'm only met with a broken shelf and shattered jewelry piled at the bottom. I sigh as I close the door, but as the sound of it shutting echoes through my head, the right cabinet door bursts open, and a giant creature grabs onto my throat. As it slowly moves out of the darkness, I see its features. The figure is a human with ashy gray fur and a nose that protrudes like a snout. Its ears stretch to the tip of the head, where they bend over, almost like a dog. The eyes glow red, and its teeth shine through its long mouth. The creature also wears a red cardigan, dark nougat slacks, and brown dress shoes.

Fancy.

"Who are you?" I ask through dry breaths. I attempt to remove its hand, but the creature lifts me into the air.

"I am from the skies you look at when the moon is out. You somehow avoided being purged thirty-six years ago, and now I am here to collect you," the dog says without moving its mouth. The voice sounds like it's coming from within my brain. The dog begins walking down the stairs, keeping me in his hand. Then, as we reach the last stair, the front door opens, and Chuck walks in with a cloaked figure covered in greasy gray rags behind him. Then, through the cloak, yellow light is barely visible.

"Perfect," the cloaked figure says. Its voice sounds electronic, almost like it was coming from a megaphone. It raises its arm, which reveals glowing yellow skin. It flexes the hand, and as its fingers open, a weird shape on the bottom of its arm starts growing. The form begins to contort into the face of Mac. It begins to bleed toward the ground, with a neck and torso following. The head opens its mouth, and the yellow color changes into Mac's skin. Arms grow out of the torso, and legs appear from the bottom as it disconnects from the figure's arm.

"Now kill him, and I will birth him myself," the cloaked figure groans. The yellow Mac on the ground grows more skin around him and clothes similar to the human Mac's produce, but this time covered in dirt and mud. It lets out a loud screech that slowly turns into Mac's natural voice.

"Calm down, Owen; it'll all be over soon," Mac's twin says, which causes my heart to drop. I wiggle around, trying to escape the dog's grasp, but to no avail. "It's an easy process, Owen. Just give your life and feel the rebirth."

"I'M COMING OWEN!" a voice calls out from the TV room. I strain my neck to look over and see Rink and The Right-Hand Man running at us. Rink jumps and flips over the railing, kicking down the dog creature, which frees me. I drop onto the ground, knocking my head against the hardwood floor. My brain spins in my skull, and I feel the world shake around me. I push myself back up, noticing the cloaked figure, the dog is gone, and Chuck is running towards the alley outside. Rink runs towards the door after him, but the Mac twin appears from the doorway and punches straight through Rink's face. The blood splatters onto the twin's arm and sinks into the skin. Rink's body falls to the ground in front of me, and the twin grabs the top of my head and pulls its arm back, getting ready to strike.

As I brace myself for death, The Right-Hand Man appears from behind the twin, pulling him into a headlock and holding up the lawn gnome Mac took earlier. He stabs the gnome's pointy hat right into the twin's left eye, spraying yellow goo all over The Right Hand Man's arms. He screams as the sludge burns through his body, melting his skin like pizza. As the rest of his body melts down, the twin absorbs the lawn gnome into its face. He grabs onto my bruised leg, which I now just notice is heavily bleeding into the wood. The twin throws me into the front yard, where I crash into an inflatable waving Santa Claus that pops and shoots air into my face. I lift my head and see the row of blue brick apartment buildings across the street and the gray, rainy sky. A drop of rain splashes onto my nose. Another hits my head.

I let out a loud cough, spraying blood onto my hands. The gradual flow of rain begins to wash off the blood from my skin. My nose starts to bleed as the rain drags the blood into my mouth. I wipe my face with my hand and look at how much blood I'm losing.

What's happening? Were we set up? Where was The Bleeder?

I roll myself off of the deflated Santa onto the wet grass. As I look up into the ever-darkening rain clouds, my head tilts towards the alley. Chuck stands at the pizza truck, handing money to some tall, frail old man wearing green jungle fatigues and a Vietnam War-style helmet, complete with a playing card.

We were set up.

"Now, you will be reborn," a voice calls from behind Chuck, who turns around and falls in fear.

"I thought I was off the hook? I did what you asked!" Chuck screams in terror as the dog man comes into my view. He grabs onto Chuck's hair, holding him above the ground, and lets out a bark that blasts Chuck's head into microscopic yellow giblets and shatters all the windows around. My ears begin to ring and bleed out as the noise most likely breaks my ear drums. The dog throws the rest of his body against the truck, which rocks back from the force, and the cutesy sign on the side is covered in yellow blood and clumps of hair. He gives the old man another stack of cash, then makes his way toward me.

Everything is sideways in my view. It looks like he's walking on the wall, even though it's just ground. The rain seems like it's coming from my left. My vision is blurring so much that it looks like I can see myself in the air. The dog man…creature…THING…continues to walk towards me as it rips a stop sign out from the sidewalk. He sticks it right in front of my face, but I am too weak to look up. All I can see are his shoes, the last thing I witness as he jams them into my eyes. One goes black, but the other is holding on, but I still cannot look up. He kicks me again, and my vision goes completely. All I can feel is him continuously kicking my face in until I lose feeling in my head. I can move my arm slightly forward, but a sharp sense of pain stops me.

I could feel something puncture my heart. My lungs stop breathing, and everything in my body stops.

Then, my breath returns, and light fills my eyes.

~~

Taking inspiration from each victim that finds themselves on Doom Land, the asylum continues to build upon itself with the fears of its captives. One such addition is in the basement, where a child's entertainment establishment was created just for a man named Nathan Redd. The asylum is owned by the sick Bone Crusher, the nude God with a taste for human suffering. The original building was only three floors tall and covered two thousand feet of the purple desert of Doom Land. The top floor is mainly used for meetings with Death, but everything else is filled with torture rooms. Everything underground, besides the restaurant, is filled with the worst terrors. Overgrown, claustrophobic, maze-like hallways guide anyone who ventures deep enough down into insanity.

The reason for the asylum is because of a trade that Bone Crusher made with Death. Any person who dies in the universe has a slight chance of being reincarnated, as before their demise, right into the asylum for Bone Crusher's collection. Death's side? Complete control of the rest of Doom Land. Of course, Death accepted the trade without hearing Bone Crusher's side. The chance of being reborn in the asylum is slim, but somehow, Owen found himself inside.

~~

The light isn't bright enough to hurt my eyes, but I still react as I see the brightness fill the space. All the pain I had just felt fizzles away within moments. One moment I was lying dead on wet grass, then the next, I'm lying alive on a dirty pavement floor. I am in some sort of cell with no apparent entrance or exit. The walls are steel and covered in all bodily fluids, male and female. A lone hanging light flickers above me and flies buzz around it, whose noise adds to the otherwise silent room. I look down at my body and notice my clothes have been replaced with a clean, orange jumpsuit. The smell of shit comes from behind me, and I hesitantly turn around to face some sort of skinny creature. Its skin is red, and it looks human, with a human shape and strands of black hair, but as it hunches down, its spine sticks through the skin in a gross way. Its skin is almost pulled over its body, with the bones being apparent. Nothing but a thin bandage of orange cloth covers his body.

I don't want to spook it, but I accidentally let out a slight cough that alerts the creature. It turns its head, and a human face stares me down with deep black eyes. Its jaw is sharp, and the cheeks are sunken in, almost becoming transparent against the darkness of its mouth. I look past the red creature to see the remains of some animal being picked apart. That's where the smell is coming from…What the fuck is that? The red man picks up the animal and holds it towards me.

"Want some?" it asks in a quiet, high human voice while chewing another bite.

"You can talk?" I ask, surprised at it being an actual human.

"I get that a lot, I am human, by the way, just very red."

"Where am I? What is going on? I can't remember a damn thing…," I interrupt. He pauses, and his eyes widen. "All I know is my name and that I'm here."

"Oh yeah. You're new-new…nobody remembers anything when they wake up here for the first time. Also,

32

this isn't my cell; I just cell hop looking for food. You're lucky I didn't pick YOU to eat," the red man says, shaking his head towards the dead animal in his hand. "But uh…yeah, welcome to the asylum. Don't expect a goodbye from here anytime soon. Nobody has ever escaped this place, and there have been some good tries over the years."

"Years?" I cut in.

"Yeah, this place is beyond our solar system, so time moves way faster on the planet, but our aging and stuff are still locked to wherever we came from. It's also surrounded by stationary vortex energy, but that's beyond my expertise."

"Cool," I say as a knock from above causes me to jump backward. I raise my hands in front of me as a small panel in the ceiling is lifted, and a light shines down. The light disappears, and then a woman drops from the hole. She lands in a superhero pose, then whips her head up and faces the red guy. Her hair is long, curly, and brown; she has ocean blue eyes and freckles covering her face's middle. She wears the same orange jumpsuit that I do. She stands up, and I walk towards her, but she spins around and kicks me in the throat, knocking me down. My windpipe aches for me to breathe, but I can't get any wind in or out. Everyone goes for the throat, it seems.

"Who are you two?" she asks, not taking her eyes off the red man.

"Why should we answer?" I finally yell out. The girl turns her head towards me and stares at me angrily. "My name is Owen, and this is…."

"Names Redd. With two D's," the red man stutters out, throwing the animal into the corner. The girl in the middle takes a deep breath, then lowers her defense. She takes a bow and snaps her fingers. The sound of rustling comes from the hole in the ceiling, and a few more people drop down. The first is a man with yellow skin, fluffy brown hair, and a lean body, just like Redd. He wears an orange suit like the rest of us. He has no shoes, and his feet are covered in scars, complete with a few missing toes.

"Name's L. She's our leader, Judith. She's SUCH a joy to be with," the yellow man sarcastically says.

"Shut up, man," Judith complains, punching L in the arm. He leads out a silent scream and pretends to punch her back. Following L, a pair of two twins drop down in unison. They both are short, plump, genderless people with green eyes, blonde hair, full handlebar mustaches, and cheekbones better than Redd's. Same orange jumpsuit as well.

"I am Aid," one of the twins says. I notice how he has a scar on his left cheek.

"My name is Den," the other twin says as they both start a handshake.

"Listen, we're going through this place looking for people to help, and for people to help US," Judith says. "I know escaping this place is hard, but I've already got this many people, so I think it's possible now."

"No, no, no, no," Redd starts yelling. "That's suicide."

"Is it better than staying here and being tortured?" Judith yells back as another girl falls from the hatch. She's as short as Aid and Den and has bluish-gray hair that ends at her waist, yellow eyes that stick out like a sore thumb, and clear skin that makes her look like a ghost. Blood-covered orange jumpsuit. "That's my sister. Her name is Cash. I want her to leave this place, even more than myself."

"I'm not trying to go out of my way to die," Redd argues.

"Fine, then don't come!" L yells out as he tries to jump back into the hole in the ceiling. "Aid, can you help me with this?"

"Will you come?" Judith asks me. I think for a moment about the situation, which I still don't fully understand. Everyone's eyes slowly stab me with the looks of anger and impatience they all have. I look at Redd, who seems to be cowering behind everyone. His arms cover the bottom half of his face, and he shivers as if he was cold. So who do I go with? I need answers; there's too much to take in right now. What is happening?

"I-I guess I'll stay with Redd," I finally let out. Inside, I could feel my inner self cringe at my decision. I should've gone with the bigger group that looks like they know what they're doing. So while Judith and the others groan in disappointment, Redd perks up and stares at me.

"You could've gotten out of here, man," Judith growls at me as her group climbs back into the ceiling. I let out a disappointed sigh as Redd crawls over to me and reaches his hand out. I stare at the red, bony hand with the metacarpals bulging through the skin. I slowly reach my hand out, and as they connect, Redd shakes it up and down.

"Thank you," he says. I let go of his hand and look at him quizzically.

"For what?"

"Most people are scared of how I look because of the protruding bones and the red skin."

"Look, man, I have no idea what the hell just happened in the past, however long I've been here, but you have been the most ordinary thing I've seen here," I say as I walk underneath the hole. I look up through the cracked, dirty tile ceiling at what looks like a utility tunnel, although the darkness obscures what I can see. I try to reach up to grab the edge of the hole as the dirty wall in front of me shakes, causing dust to fall off and onto the ground. I step backward, reaching my right arm back to feel for Redd. A bright yellow light shines under the wall as it rises into the ceiling, letting the outside view fill my eyes. A large room filled with rows of cells with one-way mirror walls, lining the barriers that continue into the darkness.

Thin metal platforms connect room to room, with a large circular floor in the middle. A tube that holds an elevator shoots down the middle of the platforms. A metal guard rail is loosely connected on the side. I take a step onto the metal platform, looking at the dirty greenish walls illuminated by yellow lighting fixtures on the ceiling. I look over the rail at the endless amount of floors below us, continuing until they fade into the void. Through the one-way mirror walls, I can see dirty cells of other different kinds of creatures. Buff snakes, faceless bunnies, and even a hairless blue monkey man with one leg and two dicks on his upper chest.

Redd joins me on the platform, and the wall closes behind us with a hard thud as it hits the ground. The crash echoes through the seemingly endless hole under us. I walk onto the bridge leading to the circular floor, quietly walking to not alert anyone that could be watching. The elevator shaft in the middle opens up as I approach it, and the sound of relaxing bells chime. A white light mixes with the yellow as the circular door opens. The inside of the elevator contrasts with the dirty walls that surround it. Clean, white padding lines the inside, and the floors are made of gray marble.

Redd and I step into the small room, and I turn to see a screen next to the open door. A face flashes onto it, and a disgusting creature turns to us while staring at a holographic sheet of paper. Its face resembles a vespid, or more specifically, a Vespula rufa. A look of yellow and black, with two large antennae sticking out. The large black eyes are indented in the head, with two small, bloodshot humanoid eyes at the bottom. Its body is covered in black leather, with silver zippers scattered throughout. The left hand that holds onto the holographic paper is a claw with two large black and jagged yellow fingers. The entire right arm is a chain that ends in a spiked metal ball.

"Name and access code," it says in a warped, translated-sounding voice. I look at Redd, who looks at me. We both shrug as the creature looks up from its paper. It makes an audible, mechanical gasp. "Who the hell are you two? How did you escape?"

"Sorry, you're uh, breaking up," I lie. I punch the screen, which cracks it, but the feed is still up. I can see the wasp man move backward to a desktop microphone past the lines. So he pushes it on and speaks into it.

"All personnel onto cell floor 38, please. We have an escape attempt. I repeat, an escape attempt," he says. The audio comes from loudspeakers outside the elevator, as well as from the screen. I look outside the elevator, and across from us is an almost hidden metal door between two cells. A small dirty window in the middle of it shows a growing silhouette approaching. The entry is kicked open, and a group of guards burst in.

They're all tall but big, fleshy creatures covered in samurai-like armor of varying colors. Their ribs are exposed but surrounded by metal plates held loosely together by black hair. Their stomachs and arms wear metal plates that also cover the lower jaw. Their faces are bear-like, with large snouts and small eyes. A pointy helmet with three points rests upon their heads. Their hands are anything from claws to hooks to blades. From above and below, the sound of doors slamming open and guards pouring around can be heard.

"Get them!" one of the guards yells out, pointing at us with thin, sharp-jointed fingers. I frantically look around for a button pad but don't see anything. All of the guards charge toward us, with some climbing up from below and falling from above. Before one can reach the elevator, however, the door inexplicitly slams shut. The elevator jolts, which makes Redd and I stumble around, then shoot up. The sounds of disgruntled guards and their metal bodies attacking against the metal walkways slowly fade as we move up.

"What happened?" Redd asks. "Did you press something?"

"No, did you?" I ask back. Redd shakes his head. I check the screen, and the wasp is gone. "Maybe it's connected to the cell wall opening. I hope up means safety."

The elevator slowly comes to a stop, contrasting the quick and jerky start it had. When it entirely ceases to move, the elevator door leisurely opens to a new room. It's small and fancy. Golden wood lines the edges of dark brown wooden walls. Rows of computers atop matching wooden tables are dispersed around the place. I step out of the elevator, and Redd follows. We both pass all of the black, empty screens. A door blends into the walls on the other side of the room. I slowly put one foot in front of the other, inching closer as screaming and loud footsteps radiate from beyond the door. I turn around to Redd, who hears it too. He stands still, slowly taking one of the keyboards and holding it above his head.

I turn back around, taking one of the keyboards as well. We both stay still as the sounds grow louder and louder until the door is blown off its hinges. It flies past us, crashing into the elevator, which explodes. The smoke fills the room, and the light from outside the doorway illuminates a group of a few dozen guards.

But it doesn't illuminate us.

—

Still breathing, dismembered guards lay across tables, dangling from holes in the ceiling and body parts scattered throughout the room. I drop my keyboard and sit on one of the downed guards.

"How the hell did we do that?" Redd asks from inside a guard's stomach that was scooped out. He eats the inside fat as the guard quietly screams through a smashed jaw.

"Who knows. Maybe the smoke helped," I say back to him. I hold up the left arm of the guard I'm sitting on, and I twist its thumb off. I throw the thumb into my mouth, chew it, and immediately regret it. The carrot-like

40

consistency and leathery skin don't go well together. So I spit it onto the ground, and Redd catches it midair. "Looks like that elevator is out of order now, too. Let's hope there are no stairs."

"Ok, I'm done eating. It's starting to rot," Redd says, crawling out of the stomach on all fours. The guard continues to silently scream in agony. I stand up and join Redd as we walk through the busted doorway into a security room with screens lining all four black metal walls. A desktop mic rests on the table, just like the one from the elevator screen. I walk to a windowless industrial door with a small keyhole under its silver handle.

I crouch down to look through the keyhole. On the other side is a long, gray wall hallway with short doors lining the walls. As I look, I see Judith and her group standing in front of a large, brown metal door. They're talking about something, but I can't hear them. So I turn around to see Redd standing behind me, hunching over.

"It's Judith and her gang," I tell him. I stand up and open the door, which makes an incredibly annoying creaking noise. Judith and the rest turn around slowly, seeing me and Redd covered in assortments of blood.

"What did you two DO?" Judith angrily yells, storming toward me. Her eyebrows sharply angle themselves.

"Woah, hey, look, it was an accident," I say, backing up and holding my hands in front of me. She grabs

onto my arms and throws me past her into the others. I
knock them all down like bowling pins.

"You somehow caused the ENTIRE complex to be
alerted to your position, and you outran the TORTURER,"
Judith yells some more.

"Listen, I think someone is helping u…," I start to
trail off as the double brown doors jolt open, dust flying
off. We all turn to face the newly opened path, seeing red
carpet-covered stairs that lead up into white light. "Wow."

"That'll lead up to the mansion floors. Where the
y'know, EXIT is," Judith points out. She walks over me,
stepping on my chest without knowing, toward the door.
From the white light, a large, cinnamon roll-looking body
stumbles its way down the stairs. The silhouette turns into
the disappointing body of Bone Crusher, whose crusty fat
toes slosh across the tiled floor. His pale yellow skin and
obese flaps of skin jiggle with each step. A broken skull of
an unknown species is tied with a thin string around his
crotch. On each nipple, two bones are tied together like a
clothespin, squishing the skin. Across the male breasts,
long femur bones circle the upper chest, held together by
still connected muscle tissue.

His face is almost covered by plump cheeks that
extend into the wide neck. A faded neckbeard and a hairy
unibrow are the only hair on him. His angled eyes are
forever squinted, thick eyelids making the sharp, feline
pupils more pronounced. A large smile molds his face into

a basket of bread rolls. The light shines onto his cracked, dirty yellow teeth; he stares at us and lets out a happy sigh.

"Hello! It seems that, despite everything I have thrown at you, the escapees have almost completed their escape!" he joyfully says in a congested voice. "Now, that is very hard to do. Few have, and you never see them again because I let them go! So, who wants to go first?"

Nobody moves until Den pushes past Judith, running up the carpeted stairs. Bone Crusher doesn't break his gaze from us. Before Den can reach the white light, two holes open up from the gray concrete walls. Then, a dozen matte-black robotic arms with sharp claws at the end shootout, with four grabbing onto Den's arms and legs. They lift him above the ground, and the screams he makes don't phase Bone Crusher. Instead, they make Judith and the rest of us horrified.

One of the other eight claws digs into the back of Den's body, cutting through his elastic skin. The screams become background noise. The blood that pours down is almost made into a silhouette by the blinding white in front of it. A second claw does the same, but it digs into the front of his body. The two claws connect in the middle, grabbing onto Den's spine. They both retract simultaneously, one ripping the upper half of his skeleton out while the other rips Den's lower half out. His deflated, boneless body flaps around like a flag in the wind.

Despite all the violence, Den still manages to make noise, but the screams now turn into pathetic droning. One

43

of the remaining unused claws retreats into the dark hole it came from for a moment, then reemerges with a newly acquired silver metal tube. It positions itself in front of Den's face, then the tube emits a short blade that's been heated up. The claw slowly pushes the blade onto the top of Den's head, cutting through his skin like cake. The knife is moved down the head, splitting in half as the blade passes through the neck. Thin strings of blood and muscle pop apart as both sides of the body slide apart.

As the blade cuts through the crotch, both sides of his body are still held up. The claws pull both sides apart, dropping some internal organs onto the stairs, and the blood blends with the red carpet. The droning continues as his heart beats, despite being disconnected from everything.

"Not done yet," Bone Crusher says, still with his back to Den. A thirteenth claw comes out with a comically large blender. The other claws throw the two halves of Den, which flop around like string cheese. One of the claws reaches in and blends them with its sharp rotating claws. The mixture turns a dark red, then into a brick brown.

Bone Crusher finally turns around, and the claws deliver him a small glass cup, and some of the Den drink is poured into it. Bone Crusher raises the glass, then pours it all into his large bowl of a mouth and licks his lips, and throws the bottle behind him.

"Put that in the fridge," he says. All the claws retract into the holes in the walls, bringing the blender with them. The spots close back up. "Not the best, but better than most escapees."

Bone Crusher walks over and picks up the still-beating heart as Aid jumps over me and runs at him. Judith notices and tries to pull him back.

"Aid!" she yells out. Before Aid can touch Bone Crusher, he reaches his arm out behind him, grabbing onto Aid's face. Then, without hesitation, he closes his fingers around his head, popping it. Then, like usual, blood flies in all directions. Aid's headless body stumbles backward, with the arms feeling around his bloody neck stub.

"All of you have been pains in my ass today," Bone Crusher says in his joyfully obese voice. The sudden sound of running footsteps echoes through the hall. One of the doors on the left side burst open, with the Torturer running in covered in sweat. His open bloodshot eyes dart around the place.

"You little fuckers," he says as his eyes land on us. Judith slaps her hand onto her face, and L swears under his breath.

"Torturer, you have found us," Bone Crusher says from the stairs. "Dispose of these vial wenches into the basement. The lowest of the floors. The restaurant."

"Of course," the Torturer says with a robotic laugh. A group of guards burst from each door, holding needles like the one from the Usnax ambulance. I sigh and let myself be put under as the rest try to put up a fight. My vision fades out, and the light disappears.

~The Basement~

My head feels wet, and my back aches in pain. I sit myself up, looking around the dark, flooded room I find myself in. I'm sitting next to a table with a moldy white cloth. The rest of the room is bare, with dark gray walls decorated with black and white squares. They match the floor under the water; black and white tiles. The only light is from a crack in the wall behind me.

I use the table to stand myself up, pushing it into the ground. I shimmy into a hole in the wall into another similar room. A dull, dark room. This one, though, is connected to a hallway that leads down to a staircase. I waddle through the water, accidentally kicking someone in the head. I look down to see L lying face down on the ground.

"I was enjoying drowning myself," he says, lifting his head. Then, I grab onto his back and pull him to his feet. "Hey, hey, hey! Hands off the merchandise, pal."

"No point in drowning yourself," someone from behind L says. I look past him to see Redd pulling himself through the water toward us. "I can't seem to find an escape."

"He's been like this since before I even awoke," L groans. He pulls Redd out of the water as I did to him. "We haven't found Judith or Cash yet."

"Have you looked?" I ask. Redd shakes his head as he stands in between L and me.

"I'm looking for an exit. I might have passed them on my way to one," Redd says.

"Where?" I ask. Redd points down the hallway to a single black door. "I'm not going in there."

"Why?" L snarkily asks. "Scared?"

"Yes," I boldly state. L scoffs and grabs onto Redd's ear, pulling him through the water toward the door. I reluctantly follow. L is the first to open the door, and Redd is the first to walk into the next room. It looks the same as the one I woke up in, with a white-clothed table. I can make out something underneath, and it looks like Judith. I walk over and pull it out.

"Hey! Who's touching me!" I hear from the body. It's Judith.

"It's just us," L reassures her. She climbs up my arm, stumbling onto her feet.

"Where's Cash?" she asks. "Have you found her yet?"

Redd, L, and I exchange glances, and we all look back at Judith.

"Well…no, not yet," I say. Judith sighs, looking down at the flooded floor. We all walk back into the flooded hallway, where a new door has appeared. It's black, with a little sign that reads 'STORAGE.' L approaches it and pushes it open. The door swings with a droning squeaking noise. I look over L's shoulder to see into a damp, dark room.

"I can't see anything," Redd says, stumbling past us. He feels around the walls for a switch but trips over a dark blob against the wall. "The hell?"

A yellow light flickers on as L finds a small wooden lever poorly connected to the wall. The light illuminates the yellow, dirty tile walls and a few robotic suits around the wet hardwood floor.

"What exactly is this place?" I ask. "Why is everything so…odd?"

"Hold on…I recognize these things," L says. He approaches the one Redd tripped on, still lying face-first on the ground. I step into the room, joining L. We both look at some shiny black, featureless husk with a spot of dried blood on the bottom of its open jaw. The shape is almost human, but it's too smooth and lacks human-like qualities besides very vague anatomy. The eyes lack any color and are a dirty white with a few water stains.

"Holy shit, I know what these are from. I worked at a kids entertainment establishment that housed these mascots," L explains. "How did they end up here?"

"There's more," Redd says, pointing from the ground to a few laid down in a pile. I walk over to the top one, pulling it into the middle of the room. The appearance is that of an anthropomorphic rabbit, a red one. It has deep green eyes, which seem to roll around the head. The damaged red plastic body is held together with loose wire and tape.

A small handprint stain catches my eye on the side of its stomach. I place my hand on top, and my fingertips touch some sort of divot in the suit. I push my fingers down, and the front casing of the stomach opens. It reveals a small, triangular-shaped orange shard of glass. I hold it up with my thumb and pointer, holding it up to the singular lightbulb that dangles from the dirt ceiling. No light shines through it. It seems to dim the light as I hold it up.

"Hey, be careful with these," L says. I throw the shard back in the empty shell, closing the stomach and pushing the rabbit aside. "Let's see who else we have."

"This one is ugly," says Redd, who has finally stood up. He holds up a human-sized sock puppet-looking thing. It seems to be two fabric suits stitched into one. The left side is a happy brown rabbit, like the red plastic one. His face has a large smile, although it lacks a lower jaw. One of the eyes is missing, and the other is just a sewn-in black button. On the other side is a sad brown bear with a large, arch frown stitched into its black face. A small black top hat made of plastic rests upon its head.

L struggles to carry another plastic one on his back, which he throws onto the red rabbit. It's an ugly orange bird with a cracked green beak and no eyes. Broken shards around its body expose peeled wires, which shoot out tiny sparks. It has long legs that end in sharp talons and short arms that are perpetually pulled back. As it falls, it clashes with the rabbit, with pieces cracking off onto the muddy ground. Redd and L stand next to me as we look at the plastic husks.

"Hey, where's Judith?" Redd asks. I look up at him, also noticing the black suit is gone.

"Where's the featureless one?" I ask, right as the lightbulb shatters. The three of us duck as the shards fly across the room. When we all brush ourselves off, we realize we are the only ones left in the room. Each of the mascots is gone. The ground also seems to be slightly more flooded than before.

"What the fuck?" L asks. He feels around his jumpsuit, shoving his hand into one of the butt pockets. He pulls out a small bronze box with an etching of a wolf creature on the side. He flips the top open and sparks a small flame. "I stole this from a guard a long time ago."

"Good thing we have it," I say. L leads the way out of the room, holding one hand over the lighter as we venture through the basement. "Let's not be too loud, ok?"

"Sure," Redd whispers. We try to avoid splashing the water too much, which proves to be a problem as the water is too deep to sneak around in. It's above our ankles now. We bump into the occasional pipe dangling from the ceiling and find ourselves back at the staircase.

"We just went into a circle?" L angrily whispers.

"Goddammit," Redd swears. L attempts to speak as a soft blow is heard, and the flame is quenched. The soft light disappears as everything is once again enveloped in darkness.

"Guys?" I ask. Nobody responds, and I feel something soft brush against my left arm. The flame appears again, and I see L's face light up. We both look to our right, where Redd is nowhere to be seen.

"Ah, shit," L says as the same blow is heard again, extinguishing the flame. I feel the lighter hit my knee, and I bend over, feeling around the water for it. My fingers grab onto something colder than the odd breeze going around. I bring it up to my face, lighting it back up. L is gone, and I wait, shaking and breathing heavily as I feel two large hands creep onto my shoulders. I turn my head and bring the lighter up to the face of the red rabbit, the green eyes being cast away in shadows. The only thing I see is the outline of the large mouth and eyes as the grip tightens on my shoulders. I scrunch down, trying to break free, but the robot pulls me back up.

"What ARE you?" I yell out. The mechanical creature bends closer, its green eyes slightly poking through the darkness.

"Want some pizza?" it asks. I scream the loudest I ever have as a rusty brown pipe is thrust from its mouth, stopping inches away from my face. My scream continues as the hands let go, and the arms fall to their side. The pipe is pulled out, and the rabbit falls onto the ground, some exposed wires almost shocking the water. I hold out the lighter to see Judith holding the broken pipe, and my scream slowly lowers into silence.

"What the FUCK!" I yell out, still shaken from the encounter. L and Redd appear, throwing the broken shells of the orange bird and black suit onto the ground. "Where's the sock puppet fucker?"

Judith pulls out the stuffed animal's corpse from her outfit, tears it in half, and lets it drop to the ground, where she then begins smashing the other plastic suits with the pipe.

"A bit of overkill, huh? They are dead now," L says as she doesn't stop until they're all broken into a hundred chunks.

As Judith shoves some of the broken robot parts into her orange jumpsuit, the sound of a creaking door grabs our attention. We all raise our arms as if to defend ourselves. A glowing red light shines down the staircase, painting the water a deep purple. Although the previously locked door is now open, none of us move. I notice a tiny white light spark from the bottom stair, and so does L.

He makes the first step, walking toward it. As he gets closer, the spark grows until it forms a physical object. The appearance is that of a small snowman plush, with two black eyes, a carrot nose, and a ripped green scarf around its neck. The snowman scrunches itself down, almost entirely underwater, then bounces into the air. The water around it is shot up as well and drenches L.

Before we can ask questions or catch the floating snowman, it evaporates into the air. Then, with wet hair covering his face, L turns around. He opens his mouth, and water pours out.

"Maybe that is who keeps saving us," I whisper to Redd. He shrugs but seems to agree. "I'm not going to question anything anymore. Let's go."

I pass by the still shocked L, who shakes his head, his hair throwing water across the room. Judith crouches to look through the door into the red light. I do it as well. Past all the red, I can see a faint white light.

"Is that an elevator?" Redd asks. I turn around to see him also crouched. "That light looks just like the one we were in."

Judith walks toward the stairs, puts one foot on the bottom step, waits for a second, and then places one on the next step.

"Why is she hesitating?" I ask L.

"You saw what happened LAST time we tried going upstairs," he responds, lifting his wet hair off his face. But, unlike Judith, I quickly walk up the stairs, my wet feet slapping against the dry steps. The red light fades away through the now open door as we all pile onto a small walkway. Then, like Redd said, an elevator like before waits for us. I look down next to the walkways, where the void awaits anyone who falls down. Above us is the ground of the lowest floors in the asylum.

"Do we trust this elevator?" Redd asks. L quickly steps into the clean, glowing lift.

"I do," he quickly states. Redd and I both enter simultaneously, and Judith is the last to follow. A screen like before clicks on next to the door, with a quick snap sound. The snowman from before appears, wearing small googly eyes and with a set of human phalanges hanging off his head like antennae.

"Hello, you four. The name's Snowman, and I'm sending you all up to the mansion floors," he says through the screen. The elevator door closes as he finishes his sentence.

"Why are you helping us?" Judith asks.

"You are not the one I can tell. But either L or Owen is the one I'm looking for, but I haven't decided yet," he says.

"Let's focus on getting out, then we can get some answers," I argue. Redd nods behind me, and the elevator kicks on. It shoots up, like before, and quickly stops. "That was a short ride."

The door opens up to a flat area of purple sand. From West to East, the ground extends until the darkness consumes it. I turn around to face the elevator, and the shaft is in the middle of two concrete walls that cover the South of the room. The ceiling is covered in circular lights, akin to an office.

We all step out onto the sand, and the elevator door shuts, and it shoots up.

"Were we supposed to get off of that? It seems there's more above us," Redd worryingly says, a shakiness in his voice.

"This place doesn't look like a mansion," L boldly states. A familiar blubber figure emerges from the North's darkness, clapping his hands. The tubby sound echoes through the void. Bone Crusher steps into the light, which illuminates his body and gives his body more shadows, which brings out his replete rolls.

"Bravo, bravo," he says. "I thought nobody could escape the basement, but it seems you four have…although one is missing. Shame."

"Where's my sister?" Judith demands. She takes a step toward Bone Crusher, and he scoffs at it.

"Hey, what's the point of this room?" Redd asks. Bone Crusher diverts his attention to him.

"It's unfinished. We're still building onto the many floors of this place," he responds. He lifts his arms up and turns around, looking at the empty void in front of us. As he's looking away, the elevator returns from above, and someone grabs onto L and pulls him in. The rest of us turn around to see Cash, bloodied and battered. She motions for us to join her, and I don't hesitate to jump into the elevator.

Redd notices and joins me. Judith is the last to see, and when she turns around, she stumbles and trips onto the sand. The impact alerts Bone Crusher, who turns around and yells.

"You won't escape again!" he yells out. Judith pulls herself forward, crawling toward the elevator. Cash pushes us out of the way, running toward her sister. She grabs and pulls Judith's arms while keeping an eye on Bone Crusher.

"Judes, go on without me," Cash says. Judith quickly looks up.

"Do you not remember the plan? You first, then me," Judith pleads.

"Plans don't work here," Cash says as she throws Judith into the elevator. Judith stands up and tries to run back, but L grabs onto her arms and holds her back.

"CASH! PLEASE!" Judith screams out, her voice cracking. Cash turns her head around and winks at Judith, who screams. "NO!"

The elevator door closes, and as it does, time slows. Judith slowly tries to break free from L. Redd grabs her arms too. Cash turns back to face Bone Crusher as he runs straight through her body. The skin and bones fly in every direction as the door finally shuts and Bone Crusher slams into it. The elevator slowly rises as Judith falls to the ground in tears.

The rest of the ride is silent as Judith lets the tears stream down her face. The only sound is the tears hitting the floor. The otherwise short trip feels like an eternity. Once the elevator door opens, Judith is the first to walk out. We enter the back half of the mansion's first floor, and the elevator is next to a large, straight staircase. It leads up into the darkness and down into the lower levels of the complex.

The walls are a clean, dark brown wood, with a few bay windows showing off the dark green sky. The room is bare, with the only decoration being a steel cabinet with sparkling blue weapons inside. I can tell there's a spear, a mace, and a javelin. The rest are otherworldly in design. The floorboards creak with each step as I walk around the room. A few doors are scattered around the room, but all are locked. A sound emerges from the lower stairs, an almost inhuman scream.

"I'm guessing we want to go up?" L asks. He walks onto the stairs, looking down into the depths. "Blood is covering the walls down there."

"Up it is," I say, walking past L. I hold onto the groaning railing, which wobbles with each step. The darkness begins to swell around me, and I feel the damp wall for a switch. My fingers pass over a small indent in the wall, activating a generator. The sound of grinding metal starts as overhead lights buzz on. The bright blue glow lights up the rest of the stairs, which continue upward. I instead turn to my left, where an open doorway leads onto the second floor.

I walk through into a void of blue. The same blue lights from the staircase are on the room's ceiling. L, Redd, and Judith walk before me, checking out the decor. A long, fourteen-feet long table surrounded by seven chairs sits at the far end of the room. The walls are all covered in a reflective material that makes the room look bigger than it really is. In each corner of the room, tall black pedestals hold ancient artifacts. Each one seems like a small rock, with holes that leak bright white light that pierces through the blue atmosphere.

From the rocks, white sparks erupt from the holes. They shoot into the air, circling around the room, getting closer and closer to each other. L puts his hand up, letting the tips of his fingers touch the moving sparks.

"I bet it's that snowman dude," Redd says. The sparks get closer until they all slam together, emitting a blinding white light that lowers onto the middle table. The light fades, and the snowman creature stands, looking at us. The room returns to blue.

"Hello, survivors," the snowman says.

"Who ar-I mean…WHAT are you?" L asks. The snowman floats into the air, hovering on L's shoulder.

"I don't have a name, but you can call me Snowman. It's what others call me," it says. So I exchange looks with Judith, who shrugs. "I'll keep it short, but I am looking for someone to help my creator, and most of you are from Earth."

"And what does that give us? Special powers?" I ask.

"No, but he believes that one of you managed to escape the very thing he's going after," Snowman explains. Redd appears from the doorway, breathing heavy and covered in sweat. "You managed to survive-well, kind of-someone of great power. As for those not from Earth, welcome along."

"I'm sure the talking snowman is great, but we have a problem," he stutters. The end of his sentence is followed by booming footsteps from below us. The walls begin to shake, and the pedestals fall onto the ground, smashing the rocks on top. Redd looks down the staircase, then quickly turns to run up. L follows him without hesitation, with Snowman holding onto the side of his neck. Then, I run over to the stairs, peering at the impending doom. I see Bone Crusher slamming his bread baskets of toes up the steps, crushing each one as he goes.

He notices me and begins to walk faster. I let out a loud yell as I turn around as fast as I can. I jump up the stairs, climbing up on all fours. The wooden stairs turn into metal around halfway up. I try to look behind me, but my head can't do it. I reach the top, launching myself onto the third floor. I roll into the others, who are huddled up against some cobweb-covered boxes.

"It's nice to know there's a spider here," L says. So I grab onto his arm, pulling him out of hiding.

"Let's go!" I yell at him. I look down a twisty, winding, dark path to my left. Redd bolts past us, running past the contorting moldy gray walls. I look back down the stairs as Bone Crusher continues to chase us. His footsteps still shake the uneven floor. I push L forward, who bumps into Judith as the three of us start running away. We travel down the dark hallway, the walls seeming to rotate, and the floors bleed under our feet. The darkness swallows all light, and soon I feel like I'm running in nothingness.

However, this feeling doesn't last for long as I crash through a wooden wall. The planks break from the impact, and I'm flung out of the mansion for a brief moment. I dare not to open my eyes, so the cold breeze is all I get as I fall through a glass roof. I land on L, who also fell. I finally open my eyes, looking up at the green sky. Dark green clouds melt together, blocking a faint light beyond the atmosphere.

"We need to make sure he doesn't jump down here, or we're all dead," Judith says, just as the familiar footsteps ring through the air. I look down at the room around me, seeing tables of unearthly plants. Vegetation with teeth, some that move by themselves, and some that grow weird-looking fruits. I look at Judith, whose jumpsuit matches her sisters, covered in blood. Her hair droops in front of her face, with patches sliced in half from the glass. I look around for Redd, who I see hiding under a giant brown leaf the size of a bed pillow. His red skin quickly hides any bleeding he has, but the deep cuts around his chest stick out easily. I look up again for Bone Crusher.

I hear mumbling from under me, and I remember I'm sitting on L. I get off, standing above him. His face stays flat on the floor for a moment. The back of his head bleeds red against his yellow skin, and I see Snowman crawl from underneath L's body. It uses its nose to pull itself out from under L's weight. Snowman looks at the broken wall to look for Bone Crusher before turning to me.

"Look, I can help you get out, but it'll be a bumpy ride, and it won't get us far," Snowman says, checking for the approaching Bone Crusher.

"Just do whatever! We need to leave!" I yell out. Snowman looks back one last time, and the ground below us begins to shake. Under each person, the wooden floor breaks itself apart and launches up through the ceiling. We're all thrown into the Roan sky as Bone Crusher curses from below, looking out from the broken wood wall. We begin to descend, falling miles away from the mansion. I see L go straight through the sand, and Redd's lower half goes through. I brace myself for impact as I slam right into a dune.

~~

The throne of Death is compiled of bones from each creature he slays off-planet. It sits in a large, castle-like building crafted by mortal slaves shackled by their legs. The castle is built from vigor-infused rock from the Inazian colony of Optinas, a race of creatures with little more than three-foot-tall eyes with legs made of the extraocular muscles connected to the sclera.

In the Hall of the Anguished, large archways hold up an impressive twenty-foot tall ceiling, and the dark gray interior makes the candle-lit rooms almost pitch black. Tall open windows blow air throughout the hall, nearly killing the candles. The significant steel portcullis is hoisted up by trapped tortured souls holding forever burning chains. The dark green outside light pours across the dark floor.

Death's eye cavities glow from the light. A stained brown cloak covers his body. He rests upon his chair, waiting as a mere mortal walks into the hall. His skin is a bright blue, with a sizable white birthmark across his eyes. His head is devoid of hair, his mouth bare of teeth. He dons a shredded orange jumpsuit. A small black box is half-stitched into the left side of his stomach, with a tube that feeds into his Adam's apple. The green light paints him a dark cyan.

"Mr. Geryo, how pleased I am to see you," Death booms, his voice bouncing off the walls. Geryo quickly falls on one knee and bows his head. Death stands up from his chair, walking down the steps that lead to his throne. He places his bone hand on Geryo's smooth scalp.

"My lord, I have come bearing news from the asylum," Geryo says. His voice was shaking like the rest of his body. Death nods as he removes his fingers from Geryo's head.

"And what is it you have brought for me to hear?" Death implores.

"There are escapees, and Bone Crusher feels the presence of a God with them." Death nods again to the information. He stands behind Geryo, who remains bowed. Death removes his hood, letting the light shine onto his yellow skull. His lack of eyes and his void-like mouth stand out.

"Perhaps he has returned," Death declares. Geryo lifts his head up and turns to face Death.

"Who, my lord?" Geryo asks. Death turns to face Geryo, who shudders in response. Death raises his hood as he begins to speak.

"Nobody that concerns you." Death walks past Geryo, back up the stairs to his throne. He takes a seat, and as Geryo stands up, Death holds his hand.

"You want me to join you?" Geryo asks. As Death's hand emits a soft orange glow, he begins to trek up the stairs. Geryo stops midway up. A smile grows across his face. "I'm pleased, my lord."

A tiny skeleton arm pops out from the hand, followed by another. They are both made of pure molten rock, with bits of lava dripping down from the joints. Geryo's smile drops. The arms hoist themselves out of Death's hand, and a mini, two-feet tall lava skeleton lands on Geryo's face. It holds onto his cheeks for support.

Geryo screams as the molten monster opens his mouth with its feet and shoves itself into his mouth. Geryo tries to pull it out, but the skeleton crawls through his throat by pulling on his tissue. His voice gets congested as the creature burns his throat, and as it goes lower, his stomach.

Death closes his hand, which eliminates the orange light. He waves at the portcullis, which promptly slams shut, echoing through the hall. Geryo falls to the ground, rolling down the stairs as his body burns from the inside out. His flesh is turned to ash, promptly blown out through the open windows into the outside.

"I want you to join the rest of your tortured kind," Death says before his body fades into nothing.

~The Awakening~

Throughout the walk, I don't make eye contact with anyone. I have one mission: to get to my job. East Usnax mall is the place to go if you want to spend a fortune on parking and not have even money to buy the groceries you came to get. The mall opens at 8:00 AM on weekdays, and I had just arrived at 7:55 AM, so I could walk in as soon as I parked. Although it is warm outside, my skin looks pale, and my usually bouncy brown hair feels brittle. I had picked some black sweatpants, a Seventh Hunter t-shirt, and my shiny red flame-striped sneakers this morning, trying to stand out from the people wearing the same boring outfits. My wife used to tell me how my dark blue eyes were enough to distract anyone, but I always thought my eyelids covered them. As I walk through the surprisingly busy mall, I pass kiosks of people trying to force me to buy cheap plushies, shoe shining services, and school supplies midway through November.

Once the autumn smell and the arcade machines' noise filled my senses, I knew I was close. I pass by Austin's Candles and Crème Brûlées, trying to walk as slowly as possible to smell all of the new arrivals. I could tell they had a surplus of pizza sauce, snowy outhouse, and crème brûlées, but a fresh smell piqued my interest. I turn around and walk into the large store, with wood shelves covering the green walls and hundreds of candles combining to create one prominent smell. At the far end of the store is the cashier, where my friend Markus is ringing up an old woman I don't know. In the front of the store are two round tables with the new releases. All the smells I had guessed were there, but the unique smell was called U. It has a gray look and a greenish undertone. I pick up the U candle and smell it, and I feel my nostrils scrunch up from the horrid smell. I throw it back down and wipe my nose, and then I sniff a few of the good candles to clear out my nostrils.

I quickly speed walk out of the store, continuing to walk towards the end of the mall, when I hear commotion from behind me. I slow my speed and turn my head, where I see two figures dressed in some sort of white hazmat suit wielding assault rifles rush into the candle shop. As soon as they disappear from my view, the sound of screaming is heard by everyone as one of the figures runs out with a smashed cardboard box labeled U Candles. They run in the opposite direction of me, but I still decide to start walking faster again. The sound of gunshots clouds the screaming, and I begin sprinting away. I'm only a few stores away from my job and from the exit as two security guards dressed in navy blue riot gear and shields run past me towards the candle shop.

This is normal for me, for everyone in Usnax. Stores were robbed all the time, and our city has always been the murder capital of the world. Usually, everyone goes about their day as someone is robbed, murdered, or kidnapped in broad daylight, but once gunshots are involved, shit hits the fan. Once I get out of reach of the screaming, I slow my speed and enter the top restaurant on the entire Eastern side of Usnax: Luva's Party World. A beautiful place full of ripped, red, cushiony booths for families to eat cardboard-flavored pizza as they watch our mascot band sing outdated songs. When I first got the job, I had to clean the black and white tiled floors, which was worse than cleaning the bathrooms.

Today is going to be a relaxing day; I already know it. I walk through the clear glass doors underneath the large logo sign, and past the diner booths and the long prize counter full of plushies hanging by their necks on zip ties, straight to the employee lounge. A small room, with a small, round gray table in the middle surrounded by three metal folding chairs, an empty vending machine, the clock-in machine, and wallpaper with different kinds of flowers hung in rows. I sit in one of the chairs and hear the front doors open. I groan and then scoot my chair back until I can see out of the slightly open employee door. As I expected, a man with pinkish skin, long black hair, skinny cheekbones, and a dull pair of greasy blue overalls walks in, holding a red triangular toolbox with a few screwdrivers hanging out of the side.

"Redd, how's it going?" I yell out. I see him place the toolbox on the prize counter table. He doesn't say a word to me and instead walks out of view. As I get out of the chair, my face turns from laughter to confusion. I walk over to the door and slowly open it more. Redd is nowhere to be seen. I walk out of the lounge into the main party area, where the main stage is covered by a red curtain with little pizza icons decorating it. Typical for pre-opening time.

I notice muddy footprints on the hardwood floor in front of the stage, leading to the middle of the curtains. I slowly walk toward it, weaving through the many tablecloth-covered tables. I put my hand on the right side of the curtain, pushing it aside. I reveal the animatronic mascots that hide behind, but also an emaciated man with red skin cowering in the corner, completely naked, with Redd standing in front of him, his back to me.

"Redd, what the fuck is happening here?" I ask, moving onto the stage. The curtain closes behind me, cutting off the primary light source. All that's left is the soft glow of the eyes of the mascots next to me. Redd turns his head around, his pink jaw is dislodged from his face, and his eyes have sunken into his cheeks. I scream in horror as he jumps toward me, and we fly into the curtains. We slam into the ground, but as I feel the impact, I feel like I have fallen through the floor.

The coarse and rough feeling of sand covers my skin. I can't see, but I can hear voices above me. I open my mouth, but the sand seeps through my teeth. Something grabs my right arm and struggles to pull me through the ground. As I'm brought into the thick, dirty air, all the sand pours off my body. I spit it all out of my mouth as well. I blink the stuff out of my eyes, the image of Redd and Judith fading into view.

"L, are you ok?" Redd asks me. He reaches out his arm and pats me on mine. I look down to examine the damage, but no scratches or scars remain. I look around the purple sea of dunes, seeing the large mansion of Bone Crusher in the distance.

"Did you two wake up under sand as well?" I ask; Redd shakes his head, and so does Judith.

"I was halfway under," Redd says. Judith points to an indent behind me.

"I woke up on top there, but only because I could feel myself sinking."

"I just had a vision of a place similar to the basement. I can't remember how it went," I say quietly, to no response.

The sound of soft crunching from behind turns us around. We face a short dune, which Owen slides down. He walks past me, and Snowman materializes on his shoulder.

"There's some building over there," Owen says to Judith. He points past the dune, which I try to look over. "It looks like a bunker."

"Well, let's go; there might be some sort of escape that way," Judith responds.

"Hold on, can't he shoot us to another planet?" I butt in, pointing at Snowman. "If he's magic, how come he hasn't just teleported us to Earth?"

"You would immediately EXPLODE if you passed through the energy field surrounding this rock," Snowman says. I angrily look at him in his black, void eyes. "That green sky? That's not clouds; that's stationary vortex energy. It's what gives us life and keeps people alive here. We need something made of vigor-infused metal to pass through unharmed."

"Exactly," Owen snarks at me as he walks back toward the dune. Judith follows closely, but Redd stays by my side.

"Are we going with them?" he asks. I stare at Snowman whispering into Owen's ear.

"Yeah," I say, marching toward Owen. As I walk over the dune, I can see the faint light of a bunker in the distance. My feet slide through the sand. A soft breeze blows through the air as we traverse the sea of purple. During the walk, my foot is caught on something. I look at the ground and see an arm poking from the sand.

"What's wrong?" Owen asks, noticing I stopped. He turns and looks at my leg, which is held tightly by the unknown arm. I crouch down, examining the six long, ligneous fingers around my orange pant leg. The brown sticks extend into two equally long bone-like trunks, resembling a radius and ulna. I pull my leg up, but the arm continues to counter my strength.

"What is that?" Redd asks. He walks next to me, holding a single finger near the arm. I reach my arm out, holding him back.

"Don't touch the stick arm," I say. He nods and pulls back his finger. I look back at Owen, who's trying to break the arm by chopping it. He hits it a few times until he shakes his bruised hand.

"It's definitely not wood," he says. Judith pushes him aside, taking his place in hitting the wood. Only this time, she tries punching it with both hands. After five tries, she manages to knock a chunk off.

"I did it!" she celebrates. Her eyebrows lower in confusion after she throws her arms up in happiness. The broken area now leaks out a dirty yellow sludge. The grip of the fingers loosens, and I rip my leg out from the arm. I hop away, making sure to stay out of reach. Judith steps over to the arm and grabs it onto the bottom, trying to pull it out of the sand.

"What are you doing?" Redd asks. We all stare as Judith pulls out a skeletal corpse. She lays the carcass against the ground, a green and brown wooden human-like skeleton with ripped gray cloth covering the chest. The skeleton is slowly enveloped by the purple sand as it sinks down. Nobody says a word after; instead, we continue walking to the building we eventually reach.

We stand at the large open entrance to the brightly lit steel bunker. The inside is bare, the only thing inside being a narrow archway in the middle of the cracked beige floor. As sounds of screeching whistle through the brisk air, we all pile into the building. Owen and I push on the side of the large concrete door to close it. It slowly slides along, scraping the muddy path along the ground. It fully closes with a slam and a shake of the building, dust sprinkling from the ceiling. We all stand around the floor doorway, which leaks a warping blue light and a burning smell.

"Well, at least we found something," I say. The light shines on the four of us, Redd's skin mixing into purple. I look at Owen to see if Snowman is here, but he is nowhere to be seen. Judith rips a strand of hair and throws it into the blue portal. As the strand phases through the bubbly archway, reverse drops of liquid float up from the light.

"It's like a gateway or something. I hope it is, at least," Owen says. "I'll go first, just in case."

"Wait!" Judith yells out as Owen crosses his arms over his chest and dives into the light. He passes through, and more drips splash up from the impact. Judith quickly follows, diving through after him. Then, I look at Redd, who subtly shakes.

"Are we going in?" I ask him.

"Shouldn't we wait to see if they're still alive?" Redd asks back. An arm shoots through the portal, grabbing onto Redd's leg. It pulls him through, and Redd screams as I just grab on. I thrust my arm out to catch him, but I end up knocking myself into the portal. I phase through the energy field, the world around me melting into neon colors that spin around until I fall onto hard ground. My eyes slowly refocus as Owen, Judith, and Redd stand over me. I sit up, examining the prismarine-colored bricks that make up the area around me. The brick floor beneath me feels moist and dripping moss line the circular ceiling. The only light source comes from a large pit in the middle of the chamber.

Owen helps me up as Judith looks down the hole. I join her, gazing down at a giant orb of yellow light.

"Where are we?" Redd asks, standing behind me.

"Some sort of…ancient temple," I say, kneeling down and wiping dust off the ground. Owen suddenly jumps down, grabbing onto the edge of the pit. "OWEN!"

"Wait, I found some broken stones that I can climb down on," he responds. He begins to move down the pit toward the distant light.

"Hey, there are some carvings here," Redd says from behind. I turn around to see him checking out an archway with a pile of rocks filled in on the other side. Along the arch, etchings of a bearded man standing over an army of skinny, skeleton-like figures. "What could they mean?"

"OWEN!" Judith screams. Redd and I quickly turn to see Judith kneeling down at the pit. We run over to see Owen rapidly falling into the light. As it overtakes his silhouette, thin streaks of yellow light crash into the edges of the pit, cracking the stones. Owen is shot out, and his body hovers to the top of the dome ceiling. Light strikes rise up the hole until they blast into Owen's body. He violently thrashes as the strikes burn his body; his clothes fizzle away as the skin melts into sludges across his figure.

"What's happening?" I yell out. Owen's body is flung into the ground, sliding through cracking bricks. He hits the wall and slumps over. I slowly approach his beaten body, avoiding the light that continues to strike the room.

"Two thousand and forty-odd years ago, my first creation failed me, but now I will come to power again. Rise, Gwyn, rise," a voice calls out from the pit. The light stops, coating the room in black, as Owen rises onto his feet. His eyes bleed orange sludge that forms a four-pointed mask over his face. His melted, nude body grows black fabric to cover itself. He carefully raises his hand, and I feel myself being brought forward. My feet slide across the bricks as I'm pulled toward him. His fingers wrap around my neck as he squeezes my voice box.

"Magona will rise. Gellax will see his creation as a son," Owen says as he throws me into the ceiling. My head slams into the bricks, and I fall onto the pit's edge. Redd runs over and drags me by my legs away from Owen. Judith runs over and attempts to punch his head from behind. As her fist touches his head, her fingers are bent backward. Owen's head twists around as Judith screams and stumbles back. The points on his mask extend and slither around Judith's head. It covers her entire face, and the screams are muffled until they are silenced as the points slither away. They reveal Judith's skinned face, with both eyes rolling out of her exposed optic cavities.

She falls to the ground, splatting against the bricks. Owen kicks her body into the pit, and his foot slices her in half. He turns to Redd and me, who huddle against the dripping wall. He angrily storms over the hole, cracks of light forming from his foot touching the invisible ground. A warping sound erupts from next to me, and the same portal from before forms in the wall next to Redd. He tries to pull me through but is lifted by an unseen force and launched through the gateway. He yells for me and reaches his arm out as he phases through.

My breathing deepens as Owen reaches me and grabs onto my neck once more. He shoves his right hand into my left eye, severing the optic nerve and pulling the orb out. He crushes the eye in his hand, and sharp stabs of pain echo through the left side of my head. I try to turn to look at the portal, which shines a deep purple. I reach my left arm out, and Owen twists it backward. The bone cracks and I let out a scream. He pulls the arm off, the skin popping with each rip. It's thrown into the pit, the light pulsing on and off.

He throws me right in front of the portal. I look up at the soft purple light as Owen grabs onto the back of my head. He attempts to rip my neck as a brick falls from the ceiling, crashing onto his head. He stumbles around, holding his cracked mask, as he trips and topples down the pit. I look back to the portal and use my right arm to pull myself through. The dark chamber contorts into colorful lights as the familiar blank warehouse forms around me.

Redd appears from behind and drags me along again, out of the large industrial door into the dark green sky of Doom Land. The cold yet coarse feeling of the sand brushes against my body. Redd catches his breath as he sets me down behind a dune. I pull myself up to catch a glimpse of the warehouse as it implodes on itself, a purple glow emitting before being overtaken by orange flames. They light up the area around us until the fire dies out. The body of Owen flies through the portal as it closes, and he disappears into the distance.

"Can you walk?" Redd asks. I look over at him as the green sky highlights his cheekbones. I feel a soft touch from my shoulder and look to see Snowman lamenting. It's head bows as his body slumps over.

"It's Magona's fault. I was warned of him by my creator. He sent me on my quest while Earth was on its two-thousandth year after the death of their fake savior," Snowman says. I look at Redd, who stares into the distance, his pupils dilated. "It's not worth the time to explain. We must return to the asylum. Gwyn cannot fulfill his job."

~The Frog~

The looming shadow of the asylum cakes over the already dark sand. The top floor has a large man-made hole through the middle window. The walls are covered in scratch marks, and the front doors barely hang on their hinges. I slowly push them open, seeing the destroyed first floor. Fancy decor such as couches, wooden tables, and paintings lay burned across the floor. Bodies of asylum victims dot the wreckage, all still breathing.

I step over dismembered arms, piles of flesh, and cracked vases to the back wall, where a long staircase awaits. It splits into two directions halfway up, leading to the second floor. The only lights on the first floor come from the second, so most of the surrounding area is shrouded in darkness. I step on the stairs, and a body falls over the upper railings. It tumbles down next to me, and it's covered in deep bleeding cuts.

"Is this place safe?" Redd asks from behind, and I look at the body again.

"Probably not," I respond. We walk up to the top of the stairs leading directly onto the second floor. The wooden stairs turn into a concrete flooring, with subtle blue carpet lining the room's edges. The walls are light brown wood, just like the first floor. Thin long lights line the walls, shining upon rows of glass cages atop wooden tables. Each enclosure has some sort of creature or animal inside. I count about seven rows across, each being fifteen tables deep. I walk up to one in the middle, and a paper label reads 'Frogger Town.' I take the glass lid off the top and look down at the swampy interior.

Two little green frogs hop around lily pads on a small lake, and one stops when it notices me. It tilts its body, and the other frog stops as well. So I close the lid and take a closer look at the paper label. Underneath the large bold text of the town name, little text reads 'Big Frog Named Gurolica, Small Frog Name B–.' The rest of the text is ripped off.

I continue to search the rest of the cases, seeing many diabolic and unbelievable creatures. Fluffy balls of varying colors with sharp fangs for legs. Human-spider hybrids with large backsides. Fuzzy animals with long fur, slits for eyes, and nineteen tail-like appendages. Floating severed arms from some pale green monster with seven fingers. At the far end of the room sits a singular wooden desk with a moldy metal folding chair. It rests before a large glass case holding some sort of preserved beast. I walk past the messy desk and the sweat-covered chair to get a better look at it.

The creature stands in an A-pose, its arms at its side and the legs shoulder-width apart. A cracked, melted dark green robotic husk covering fleshly peach-colored insides that appear to be breathing. A small jar with a blue crack inside and a large black jagged wooden staff is trapped in the glass next to him. I try to move closer to get a better look, but Redd stops me.

"There are some interesting papers on here," he says. I turn around, and Redd flips through the mess on the desk. I walk over to him, and he hands me one. "Letters from someone named The Star."

"It's written in a language…I can't read this. How can you?" I ask. The paper is dotted with strange symbols and shapes.

"It's simple. A few symbols repeat, meaning they have to be vowels, or like P," Redd explains. "I haven't solved it all, but I found out the A are these odd triangular shapes."

He points to one of the symbols on my paper, a triangle with a line next to it.

"You can keep looking around while I translate these."

"Just watch out for Owen," I say to him. I walk back to the room's entrance, past the cages. Then, as I walk down the blue-carpeted stairs, whispers begin to rise in volume from below.

"Where the fuck am I?" I hear someone say. I inch past the ground of the second floor, keeping out of the way as I look down into the main lobby. A figure in an orange jumpsuit walks over the dead corpses and destroyed furniture.

"Hey!" I yell out. The man jumps and swiftly turns to me. He reaches at his side, feeling for something. "I'm not going to hurt you."

"Who are you? What is this place?" he asks. I hold my hands out in front of me as I slowly walk down the steps into the main area. His face is old and wrinkled, with silver hair and a sharp jawline. His eyes are as blue as an ocean.

"Listen, are you from Earth?" I ask as I step onto the floor of the lobby.

"Y-yes," the man stutters.

"So am I. Usnax? I lived there," I say. I can see that the man calms down inside. His eyelids slightly drop. "I can help you. I am with someone else, and we are trying to leave this planet."

"Who killed all these people?" he asks. I look down at all the bodies, which aren't breathing anymore. The blood dries up on the ground, and the eyes of the corpses turn a dull gray.

"Redd?" I call out and hear footsteps up above as he appears from the stairs.

"What? Who's that?" he asks, seeing the man.

"They're dead," I say.

"Yeah, I know," Redd responds. He walks over to the man and looks at him. I grab onto his shoulder and turn him around.

"No, they're DEAD, dead. Look!" I point to one of the bodies, which was immolated. The body remains still, and Redd's eyes expand. He steps back, accidentally stomping through a body's decomposing jaw.

"I managed to translate everything. You need to see it; I think I know how to get off this planet."

"Redd, are you sure it's a good enough way?" I ask. He hesitates and nods his head. His eyes remain on the burnt body, its mouth wide open in a never-ending silent scream. We walk back up to the desk, where Redd sits in the dirty chair. He sets his head down on the table.

"Are you ok?" the man asks Redd.

"Give him a moment. He's a little shaken," I say, holding an arm out between the man and Redd. "While we wait, who are you?"

"You can call me Nolen. I can't really remember what was happening before I appeared here," the man says. "I was with a group of people and then... I'm not sure."

"I've been here a while. Jumped from group to group, not really being able to find my place," I say. "Ok, buddy, we need some information now."

I pat Redd on the back, causing him to jump and knock some papers onto the ground.

"Sorry, I am just a little scared of bodies like that," he says. His voice shakes. "Anyway, these are from The Star. It seems to be a being of cosmic power, like Bone Crusher."

"Are they like...love letters or something?" Nolen asks. Redd takes a shredded yellow-stained paper from underneath a pile, handing it to Nolen.

"It's very vague, talking about hatred for what he calls 'Replicate.' I'm not sure what-or who-it is. He doesn't go into detail," Redd explains. "But he is on Earth, this star man. He calls it the second Earth, which doesn't make any sense."

"We're a second Earth?" I ask.

"I might have translated a few words wrong," Redd says. "But whoever this star man is, he has suspicions about someone. So I can see the writer is trying to explain how they believe the 'Replicate' wants his rebirthing energy for an army, by building one themself."

"So should we be worried about this 'Replicate' character?" I ask. Nolen squints his eyes and looks closer at the paper. His eyes widen.

"Jesus Christ. I know who wrote this," Nolen blurts out. His fingers let go of the paper, which floats down onto the desk. "He's an enemy of a long-gone teammate."

"He is on Earth?" Redd asks. He stands from his seat, the moldy chair falling onto the ground. Nolen nods his head.

"I had to work with him a few times, just to guarantee my safety, and he double-crossed me," Nolen explains. A loud crash from a distance breaks up the conversation. We all turn our heads to the entrance to the room, where a decapitated head rolls in. I slowly approach it, Nolen moving faster than me. He picks up the flabby orb, parts of tissue and spine poking out from the shredded neck. The drooping cheeks and oily skin stand familiar; Bone Crusher.

"Who's this?" Nolen asks. I slap the head out of his hand. It hits the ground with a soft plop, blood splattering against the tables and glass displays.

"Someone that I didn't think could be killed," I say. I look into the darkness of the doors, attempting to see where it came from. Redd taps me on my shoulder, and I turn around.

"If he's dead, then we know who did it. So we need to get back to Earth," Redd says. I slightly turn my head.

"Redd, we tried to get back to Earth. It did not work," I say to him. Redd smirks as he taps his dome with his pointer fingers.

"I know who to ask," he says. He cups his fingers around his mouth. "SNOWMAN!"

Snowman quickly pops into the air from a small blue light. His dark black eyes have little red lines sprouting from them. He hops around in thin air as he stops on Redd's nose.

"WHAT!" Snowman yells, his voice shaking the room and cracking some glass. The cage holding the figure in the back develops a large webbed crack on the front. Redd's ears begin to bleed as he blinks his eyes from the severity of the sound.

"Did I wake you up or something?" Redd jokingly asks. Snowman's eyes squint as he smashes his little soft head into Redd's forehead. "Do you know any way to get to Earth? I don't know why we haven't asked you yet."

Snowman slowly hovers away from Redd's face. He lets out the beginning of a word as the lights flicker. The cages and glass begin to bend and shatter as the entire room shakes more than before. Snowman pops out of existence as we all lose our balance and fall onto the hard ground. The ceiling above us cracks and fractures as it is raised above the walls. The green light from outside fills the room as we scramble to crawl out of the way of falling glass and rocks. Nolen pushes his arms against the shards as he reaches the doors first. Redd climbs on my back as I escort him through the dangerous rain of debris.

We make it to the exit as the ceiling is dropped onto the room behind us. We all lay down on the carpet stairs as we see the corpses below us from before. Redd hides his eyes with his hand as one of the bodies crawls up the steps toward us. It's a legless green chest with yellow infected blood streaming down from a testicle-stuffed mouth on a barbed-wire-covered face. It uses both arms to pull itself up, but I quickly extend my leg above it. Finally, I stomp my heel into his back, the contaminated blood squirting as the plasticky skin breaks under the hit.

None of us speak as we walk over the bodies lining the lobby. Instead, we just focus on getting to the doors as the building shakes and loud noises boom below us.

~The Proposal~

As we walk out of the mansion, the green sky brightens. The forever night turns to day. I push open the front doors, which promptly fall off their hinges. They hit the ground with a slam, and dust flies off. From beyond the dunes, a shadowy figure looms. It fades into the shining sky before I can point it out to anyone.

"I think I saw someone," I say.

"Probably just a sand tornado," Nolen guesses. "Do those happen here?"

I take a few steps into the light purple sand as the figure appears again, this time on a dune a few feet in front of me. A brown-stained cloak flows in the stiff wind. The legs that extend to the ground are cracked yellow bones.

"Hello? May we help you?" I ask. The figure doesn't respond. Instead, it points at Snowman.

"You know he won't return until his job is done, right?" Snowman asks. "As long as he is still alive."

"What's going on?" Redd inquires from behind. The figure finally speaks.

"What are you looking for?" his crackling voice demands. Snowman bounces off my shoulder and hovers over to him.

"The TV believes that one of these humans can help. He wants some defense against The Star-" Snowman starts.

"No, no, no," the figure cuts in. He shakes his hooded head from side to side. "Go back and tell that old man to let it go. They are both building an army because they think the other is. I can't even remember who started this 'war.' The TV is just going to frighten The Star if he meddles with their affairs. I will continue to not care about anything, as long as it means I'm not pushed into anything."

"You seem to care if you came all this way to meet us," I cut in. The figure looks toward me and removes its hood, revealing a yellow skull with no eyes. Its jaw hangs partially open.

"I was told a God was with your group, believing it to be The TV back from his little planet-saving mission. He's in over his head; they all are," the skeleton says. "Knowing it's just his little minion makes this journey pointless. Do any of you know what you're getting yourselves into? You are in the middle of a war for defense, and the sides you are fighting for are both confused about their roles."

"I'm just here cause they helped me escape," Nolen says. He shrugs his shoulders and backs up a few steps.

"We're only here because the Snowman helped us escape," Redd and I say in unison. "I am helping him with his goal while it helps us with ours."

"Pathetic. What did you do with Bone Crusher?" the skeleton booms. His shadow grows in size as the light from above lowers to the horizon.

"He's dead," Snowman says. "Killed by the risen Gwyn."

The figure seems shocked, his jaw hanging wide open, and he takes a step back and looks down.

"H-how?" he stutters. "The Angelic couldn't have possibly-"

"It's obvious, isn't it?" Snowman asks. "The Angelic found a way to bridge a gateway to the tomb. It's a matter of time until Gwyn awakens Magona. Everyone will be enslaved, and we'll be on the chopping block, just like The Seventh Warned."

The skeleton stares at Snowman for a long minute; the silence is louder than words.

"Magona cannot be brought back. He exists in the Plane of Celestial. The tomb is destroyed, and his spiritual being cannot fulfill your twisted thoughts. I'm not getting involved," he finally says, raising his hood over his head. "I'm not getting in anyone's way. I have never wanted more than I already have. It is the downfall of beings with power."

The skeleton begins to fade, his legs turning invisible at first but stopping as something pierces his body. We all look to see a long, glowing blue spear through the bone and cloak. The spear is then thrust upward, slicing the skeleton in half. Both sides of the bony figure fall onto the soft sand.

From behind, another figure appears, donning a black poncho, black bodysuit, and an orange mask with four points that extend in each corner. He holds the blue spear and, as one half of the skeleton tries to reach out, stabbing the sharp end into its ulna. Rainbow lights begin to shine inside the skeleton's cloak, forming together and slithering into the other figure's mask. Each point on the mask grows sharper and begins to bend backward.

"Is he awakened?" Snowman asks. The figure reaches his arm out, which stretches and grabs onto Snowman's lower half. He retracts his arm, bringing the helpless minion to him.

"Give him back!" I yell out, running toward him. The figure looks at me and crushes his fist without saying a word. Snowman's lower half pops, and the head shoots into the air, where I jump forward to catch it. It lands in my outstretched arms as I land face-first into the sand. I look back at the figure, who stretches his hand out again. But this time, white light comes out and surrounds me. I suddenly feel myself move in every direction, my soul almost separating from my body. The white light begins to move around me in circles, getting faster and faster. My voice starts screaming as everything becomes too much, and my vision goes black.

"WAKE UP!" someone yells. My eyes quickly open, and I jump up. I look forward to see some brightly dressed man pointing a pistol at me with both hands on the handle. I look down to see I'm on top of some silver desk, and a bunch of old computers have fallen next to me. The man walks to my right, still pointing his weapon at me. His outfit is a bright yellow jumpsuit, with large red letters on his chest reading 'RUYNM.' His face is nothing special; a shaved, round head, a nose with enormous nostrils that point forward, a mouth with small lips, and pale skin.

"Where are we?" I ask, my voice slow and droopy.

"How did you get here?" the man asks, his voice deep and crisp.

"We were teleported, I think," I reassure him.

"Where does your group hide?" he demands, shaking his gun as he speaks.

"Group? What group? The hell are you talking about?" I ask in heavy confusion. The man doesn't respond, so I look around the room. From the looks of it, the place seems to be some sort of liar. Screens displaying static cover one entire wall, and the dim lighting barely shows the peeling red flower wallpaper. Behind the coverage are greasy gray walls. "Is this Earth?"

"Yes," the man finally says.

"I am from here," I respond back.

"So am I!" I hear from yonder. I look past the yellow-suited man to see industrial double doors being opened by Redd, who runs in. The man re-aims his gun away from me and toward Redd, who comes to a stop when he notices.

"And where did you two come from?" the man asks.

"Roan," Redd responds. The man lowers his pistol and takes one hand off.

"Impossible. Matthew said it was impossible for humans to come back when I first met him," the man says. "He talked about it almost every day until a few years ago. How did you all escape?"

"We were teleported by a…friend. No Nolen?" I ask. Matthew and Redd both shake their heads. Suddenly, a ringing sound erupts. I turn to the man, who takes out a small black box from his back left pocket. He takes a look at it and puts it up to his ear. He walks out of hearing range, and we can't listen in.

"What is that?" Redd asks.

"I have no idea," I respond. The man nods, putting the device back into his pocket. He walks past us toward the double doors.

"Where are you going?" Redd asks.

"I have some business to take care of. Don't blow up the place when I'm gone," he says as he walks past the doors. Once he's out of view, I sit at one of the computer-covered desks.

"Redd, do you think we will ever find Owen?" I ask him. "I don't want Magona or whatever to be awakened. We should stop it, even if we aren't sure how."

"You think there's a way to stop it?" Redd asks as he sits down in a spinny chair next to me. I shrug my shoulders, placing my right arm on a random keyboard. As my skin presses against the keys, all the screens around the walls and the desks switch on. I jump in response, the sudden switching frightening me. They all switch to views outside the current room. Black and white screens of empty, hole-filled roads, half-destroyed buildings, and scattered bodies.

"Security cameras? The quality is much better than when I worked with them," I say. I look at each one, trying to search for a possible spotting of Gwyn. "I mean, he couldn't have just left us here on purpose, right?"

I look at Redd, who stares at me with a confused look.

"You don't think we were sent here on purpose...do you?" he asks. I shake my head as I realize the stupidity of the thought. All the screens remain motionless, with nothing but the occasional falling rock or flash of an animal. "L?"

"Yeah?" I ask, coming out of my concentration. I look to see Redd holding his stomach with his arms.

"I don't really feel well," he says. "I think it might be from the cross-space traveling we have been through."

"Is it your stomach, or do you feel sick everywhere?" I ask.

"I wouldn't call it sick. I just feel like I'm disconnected from my own body."

"Listen, I want you to stay here, ok?" I say; Redd begins to shake his head.

"No, no, NO, you are not going anywhere right now," he starts to plead. "Goddammit, L, at this point, let's wait for Death to come pick us up. He had a point back there. We don't know what we are doing. Maybe being back here is a sign to stay the fuck out of it all."

"Redd. What if we don't die before we are enslaved by Magona?" I ask.

"Do you even know who the fuck Magona IS? What if this is all a lie," Redd yells. His already tomato skin deepens in color. He slams his skinny arms onto the keyboards, which causes the screens to flicker with colors. They reflect off everything in the room, and we look at each other's colorful expressions. "We could wait for that guy to come back. He sounded like he knew something."

"Who are you two?" a voice calls from behind. I turn to see the blinking screens shine upon a tall, dark, malnourished man with long, snow-white hair and blinding neon green eyes. He steps in with a blank expression and a limp to his step; his body is supported by a fashionable gold walking stick. He wears a modified astronaut helmet with little boxes and tubes around it.

"I could ask you the same thing," I say, standing up from my chair. I turn my head and give him a side-eye. "And you should go first since you're obviously from a different planet."

"And what makes you say that partner?" the man asks, his eyebrows arching. "Is it the eyes?"

"No, I don't think anyone would still want a golden cane if they were from Earth. And your glowing eyes seem otherworldly," I say. "Also, the orange jumpsuit."

I point out the ripped, stained orange Roan jumpsuit he also dons.

"I found this from someone outside. Thought it looked nice," the man says. "Anyways, back to my question. Who are you two?"

"Just two humans," Redd says. "Doesn't matter at this point."

"Sorry to hear that, but I really don't care. Do either of you have any fuel? I kind of crashed here trying to get to Saulto's," the man says. "I doubt you would, though…."

"No, the only way I know how to get to Roan is to die," I say. The man awkwardly smiles and slowly backs out of the room. He walks into the double doors and out of view. "Now look, maybe HE can stop Magona and Gwyn. Happy now?"

Redd looks down and turns away from me. I direct my attention back to the screens where I can see the face of Gwyn staring at each one, even as they switch to different views.

"What the hell?" I yell out as I back up into something. I swiftly turn to face Gwyn's masked face. The four points are even more jagged now than before, and the void-like black eyes seem more profound. His black cloak also appears to be darker and extends past the feet.

"I thought I would never find you," he says, his voice mixing Owen's and a deeper, more sinister sound. "I was still learning…but now I am but a prodigy."

"Why did you come back?" I ask, my words stuttering out, one after the other. He turns his head to look at me, the black eyes creeping wider.

"I want you to witness the awakening of Magona," Gwyn booms. "I have seen through my mind's eye…the words of Magona. The future. A universe reunited with its father. A true power. An army."

"And why us?" I ask once more.

"We have ties."

"Owen is still in there, isn't he?"

My question is only met with the world around me melting into blinding lights and the feeling of my body breaking away from myself.

~The End~

Restraints around my arm and legs restrict my movement, and something over my mouth muffles my speech. A blindfold covers my only eye, but I can see the light shining. My ears pick up some speaking from all around me, but the language is incomprehensible. I try to speak again, but my screams go unheard. Something slimy touches the side of my face and rubs my cheek.

I feel the moist feeling move up to my eyes, where the blindfold is pulled off. Above me is an overhead white light, which blinds me for a moment. It's pulled out of the way, and a group of creatures stands above me. They all look like squids, with two bulging eyes on the sides of their enlarged purple heads. From the mouth area, tiny tentacles wiggle around, covering a teeth-filled hole.

More enormous tentacles burst from the sleeves and pant legs of their doctor uniform, flopping around as they move. They each hold gleaming silver tools, each sharper than the other. I try to squirm free, looking all around the blinding white walls of my tomb. The creatures hold me down, making sure I can't move. One pulls out a dirty yellow syringe and attempts to stick it into my arm, but I break the restraint and punch toward it. They all begin to speak in their weird language as I swing my arm around.

"Calm down, calm down," Gwyn's voice calls out. I shoot my head around to see him standing over my body.

He ushers the tentacle creatures out of the room. He rips some sticky paper from my mouth. "You will not have to wait much longer…Magona will soon be here."

"Owen, please, don't let Gwyn control your mind!" I yell out. Gwyn holds out a hand to my face.

"Owen? Owen is not real. Owen does not exist. Owen…he…," Gwyn pauses. His blank eyes stare into mine. His hand lowers. "Is not worth saving. You only knew him briefly, and you think it's worth it?"

"And he was innocent. YOU…are not," I say back. Gwyn turns and storms out of the room right as I undo the restraints on my legs and stomach. I hop off the soft mattress onto the hard tile ground. Everything is a shiny white, even in the outside hallway, which leads into dark voids on either side. The walls are lined with different doors with little silver numbered signs. From the darkness, I hear footsteps which are followed by Redd on my left.

"He came into my room after," he says. "I think Owen is still there; why else would he have let us out that easily?"

"Let's hope it's easy to escape, as well," I say. "Which way?"

"There was a large window next to the door I emerged from," Redd says. "Maybe that could work?"

———

I look out the large stained glass window. The design is of a creature with an elongated skull, with the sides wrapping around the jagged jaw. Its eyes bend around a large slit in the middle of the face, and long, muscular arms end in sharp, barbed fingers. The window is split into multiple little colorful pieces, all welded together to form a large image.

Through the glass, I can see a large gray chamber with purple vines crawling along the walls. Corpses wearing familiar orange suits line the ground. Dim lighting peaks through cracks in the ceiling. Gwyn walks into view, carrying a pile of blooding scrap. He throws it in the middle of the room and kneels.

"Magona. The body of The Angelic shall be given new life," Gwyn says. A silhouette of gleaming blue light emerges from the slabs of skin and meat. It towers above Gwyn's kneeling body, and the body parts float and sloppily connect. They form into a body of a wrinkled, old pale man with missing teeth and deformed bones. He opens his eyes, revealing deep black holes with green slime oozing out. His cheeks sink inward, and large gaping holes expose his toothless mouth.

Cloaked figures appear from behind, carrying large mechanical objects and robes. They connect tubes to the holes in his cheeks, which fasten onto a large pack that sticks into his back. Harsh, crackling breathing starts as the pipes expand and contract with his wheezing. The figures line his body with similar black robes to Gwyn. The body looks around the room with its empty eyes and horrific breathing. His wide-open mouth drools with green sludge and raises his disfigured arms as Gwyn stands on his feet.

"My lord, we are currently searching for the almighty Tophet Sword. We are so, so close. We have sent Lord Dayag out to the moons of Loca in search of one of the pieces," Gwyn says, keeping his head down. He holds out a small piece of wood wrapped in some fabric. The old body slowly takes it from Gwyn, observing it.

"Good, my son. You will go and kill those two survivors…and make sure The Star, The Dog, and The TV perish on Earth. You have already dealt with The Crusher and Death."

"Yes, my lord," Gwyn responds. He turns to walk away, but the old man speaks.

"And make sure The Seventh is still imprisoned. Gellax will see ME and grant me the ultimate power…I will become one over all and The Cult of Magona shall breed new life!"

Gwyn nods as he continues his walk out. I turn to Redd, his face pressed against the window, his breath fogging up the glass. I tap on his shoulder.

"Doesn't seem like that's any good," I say.

"You think?" he snaps back. "The best thing would be to trick Gwyn into sending us somewhere…like when we got to Earth?"

"It's risky, but…we can try," I say, turning around to find Gwyn standing at the edge of the light, almost blending into the distant dark. The points on his mask bend inward, creating a talon-like shape.

"He has advised me to end your suffering," Gwyn booms. The voice echoes through the hallway.

"You'll be ending Owen's suffering," I say, standing my ground as Gwyn slowly walks toward me. The darkness follows behind him as the mask pulses like a heart. I run up to him, closing my right hand and pulling my arm back. I slam my fist into his mask, creating a large crack in the middle. It arches into the eyes, and one of the points breaks off. Gwyn's robes fall off, leaving only a skin-tight black suit left. I can see the mask start to fall off, and Gwyn quickly holds it up with his hands.

"NO! You are too late!" Gwyn yells. He tries to keep the mask up as the cracks grow more prominent. "You'll keep trying, but I just…please just stop."

"What?" I ask. I lower my guard from the rudeness of his change in voice. Gwyn holds up one arm, and the world melts, all except for Gwyn, Redd, and I. Everything swirls into large lights, which then combine into white.

Just as the white light appears, it fades. The sound of chirping birds and the soft blow of the wind follow the view of substantially tall snow-topped mountains. Giant sequoia trees surround the clearing I find myself in. I've gotten used to the constant teleportation at this point. Redd lays his hand on my bad shoulder, patting it as well.

"You look older," Redd says. I look at him and notice his skin looks more faded and stretched out.

"So do you," I say back.

"Why are you doing this?" Gwyn says from behind us. I slowly turn around to see Owen holding onto his bleeding cheek, slightly crouched over. His hair has gone gray, and his melted skin droops down with wrinkles. Even his black clothing is now faded and matches his hair. He steps forward, accidentally crushing his already cracked mask under his foot.

"I want to save you," I say. Owen lets out a small laugh, shaking his head side to side.

"Look at us," Owen says. He points at me with his free hand. I look at my worn body. "You're missing an arm and an eye, and I couldn't stop Gwyn myself."

"In the end, nobody ever wins. All we can do now is rest," I respond. Owen shakes his head again. He removes his hand from his cheek, which has stopped bleeding. He straightens his back, his spine cracking in the process.

"One of us has to die. And I think it's obvious who," Owen says. So I nod my head in agreement.

"I know."

"Please be forgiving."

I reach out to Owen, grabbing his neck with my only hand. I slam him to the ground, wiping his face on the dirt, which creates a small imprint on the floor. I let go just as Redd stands back. Owen rolls onto his back, looking into the sky. I look up as well to see a long, rectangular shape in the atmosphere. It slowly travels through the clouds, passing through the sky.

"Who could that be?" Owen laughs as he chokes up blood. I shrug my shoulders as I bend over, grabbing onto Owen's right shoulder. I pull him up onto his feet and then sock him in the stomach. He retracts from the hit, stepping back over the green grass.

"I don't want to kill you, but it's the only way. I wish I could bring you back," I say solemnly. Owen falls to his knees, still holding onto his stomach. He looks up at me, and his dirty and bloody face can't hide the look of horror he has on his face. He removes his hands, and I look at his abdomen. A rib around the middle of his chest is sticking clean through his skin, dripping blood.

"My...h-heart...," Owen says, blood filling his mouth. I blink my eyes, tears forming in the corners. He looks down, still having the same horrified look like his body jolts, falling to the ground. I quickly run to catch him, holding his body in my arm. His whole body shakes as if freezing, and he curls up toward my chest.

"I am sorry," I say as I quietly lay him down on the warm grass. I feel a tear fall down my left cheek. I stand up as I watch Owen's body cease to move. I bend over, closing his eyelids with my fingers.

"You did it," a cavernous voice says from behind. My head swiftly turns to see a cloaked figure standing next to Redd, who stands covering his mouth with his hands. I try to speak, but my mouth starts shaking. The figure removes its hood to reveal Death, his skull together with a rope through the eye cavities. His damaged ulna is repaired with a few staples.

"How are you here?" I manage to say. Death walks next to me, looking down at Gwyn's body.

"My soul cannot be killed. The energy that makes me a being still lives on to finish its job," Death responds. So I turn my head toward Owen.

"Put him somewhere good, please? And forgive him," I ask. Death says nothing, instead nodding his head. He holds his right hand toward Owen, whose body slowly fades into the air. Under his body grows a patch of purple lilac flowers. Death lowers his arm, and he too fades away.

"L?" I hear Redd ask. I stand up and turn my head toward him.

"Yes?"

"Tell me again, why did you want to save him?" I stand for a moment with the answer in my head.

"That orb…it had some sort of power. It did something to him. Sure, he was a bit angry sometimes, but not like how he was after that tomb. I thought I could bring him back, give him his old life again," I explain. "I knew he wasn't bad under that mask. I don't know what I had to do, but maybe I could've found out."

"I'm sorry you couldn't," Redd consoles.

"No, it's ok. It's over now. He's free."

I walk over to Redd, putting my arm over his shoulders. We both begin to walk through the immense forest surrounding us, through the trees. The sunlight shines through the thick overhead leaves, shining onto the flowers and wildlife that roam the area. I notice Redd's eyes droop down, and his body falls forward. I hold him up, helping him walk over to the nearest tree. He falls down, sitting against the trunk. His eyes try to stay open as the rest of his body limps.

"Redd?" I ask. I crouch in front of him, to which he wraps his arms around me. I put my arm around him, holding each other for a moment. His arms slowly slide down, hitting the grass. I lean back, seeing Redd's eyes are fully closed. I hear a branch crunch behind me, but I don't bother to check. Death comes into my view, and he pats my shoulder.

"I am sorry, L," Death says, with a harsh tone of sincerity. "You saved us."

I don't respond. I just wait in the flowers, waiting for the inevitable. Death removes his hand from my shoulder, holding it out toward Redd. I close my eyes as he fades away. I open them to see pink chrysanthemums dotted over the tree. Death lifts his hood as he walks out of my view behind me.

I look into the sky at the yellow sun. It shines onto my face, warming it up. As I watch up above, the blue sky turns orange. I slowly lay my back on the ground as Death holds his hand over me.

~The Home~

"Heroes are not supposed to be whom we fear. Our world President uttered these words as the state of our world fell thirty-six years ago. Although some of us have remained untouched by the mysterious mind change, the government still believes all people with strange powers to be dangerous. Since then, I have been hidden along with six others. As far as we know, we're all that's left. Forever stuck at the same age we were when it first started. All we can remember is an explosion, then waking up.

Seventeen hours ago, I picked up a colony of men and tanks about thirteen klicks west of our location. None of us are sure if they know we're here or it's just a scouting mission.

The one that formed this group is Nolen Lancaster, also known as The Bleeder to us. He's gifted with the ability to bend his own blood any way he wants. They can be used however he pleases. He can make his own liquidated blood into solids or gasses, which rarely comes in handy. He's able to quickly produce more blood to cover any losses.

The other six of the group are Nexgas, Heaven's Eye, Blue Jay, Box Master, TV-Man, and me. I am The Mouth, but my real name is Harvey Marks. I can stretch my mouth as much as I want and swallow anything with a pulse. That's really it. Blue Jay's name is Maya Patel, and she has the wings, beak, and light blue and white feathers of a traditional bird. All she can do is slightly fly and poke people's eyes out.

As for Nexgas, Heaven's Eye, and Box Master, we don't know their names. All we know is that Heaven's Eye has the power of a God, and the Box Master doesn't contribute to the group. But The Bleeder insisted he joined all those years ago. And as far as TV-Man goes, he's been gone for about ten years. He showed up one day and joined the group, discussing an army he was assembling. After a few weeks, he disappeared into the Wasteland's barren desert.

"Are they outside?" I ask, worryingly staring out of the bunker window. My reflective red and white striped outfit and dark blue shoes could have me spotted immediately by the incoming army.

"They aren't coming for us, dude," Nexgas says from behind as he shoves a burnt blueberry muffin into his mouth. His dark black industrial outfit covered in dangling wraps and ripped cloth starkly contrasts the bright yellow lightning symbols across his chest. They occasionally glow, and I believe they correlate with his power. He pushes me out of the way as he looks out the narrow window. The view only shows the moonlit orange sand dunes of the Wasteland.

"Guys, Heaven is getting some footage from the Usnax border," Maya yells from below. I turn around and run down the seven flights of ever-breaking concrete stairs to the underground safety bunker. I walk through vegetation that's been reclaiming its property for years. I enter one of the rooms, the dimly lit server area full of cameras for Heaven's Eye to manage.

Maya and Heaven's Eye are hunched over a screen on top of a silver metal table, which displays footage from outside a fence two klicks from us. Several tanks sporting a large yellow star on the side slowly crawl along the barren orange desert. Maya stands up and hands me some yellow papers. She removes thin-framed glasses and puts them in a breast pocket on her jumpsuit.

"They're just like Matthew described," she says. The Matthew in question is what name TV Man adapted after being with us for a while. It was easier than calling him TV Man all the time. So I grab the papers from here, seeing scribbles and drawings in shiny black ink. Writings of terrors and nightmares form into incomprehensible thoughts.

"Am I supposed to know what this says?" I ask. Maya groans as Heaven's Eye begins to punch the monitor. "What are you doing?"

"The feed is being lost," he says. So I crouch down to look at the screen, which flickers with static. "I can't even switch it to show outside our doors."

"Harvey!" Nexgas yells from outside. As I walk out, I toss the papers onto Heaven's Eye's lap. I traverse up the staircase until I reach the large bunker door. Nexgas stands with his hands on the glass, staring out as a yellow light shines through. We both react, holding our arms in front of our eyes. I feel someone push on my left shoulder, and I open my eyes to see Nolen walking toward the door in dark green fatigues, a gray metal helmet, and his signature frail body. He sets his palms on the door and pulls it to his right.

"Hey, Nolen, what are you doing?" I ask. He doesn't answer. "Nolen?"

Once the door is open, the light of a dozen spotlights blinds us again. My eyes focus on large deep green military tanks with faceless guards in sand-colored armor. Atop the tanks are large man-handled turrets pointed right at us. Helicopter blades drone into my ears as a few fly down from above.

"Hey! Hey! They're in here!" Nolen yells, running out into the spotlights. I turn to Nexgas, both of us stricken with terror. Nolen yells into the middle ground between us and the tanks, trying to make small talk with the armed men. "How much do I get for this? It's an entire team!"

"Good job, my friend," an echoing voice says from the air. "But I told you to bring me The TV."

"They can help you find him!" Nolen yells out, his voice slightly afraid. A small, four-pointed star spins around the distant sky, and a blue-suited body appears from behind. It walks on thin air down to Nolen, holding its arms behind its body.

"You found me when I was just a burning body of stellar power," the yellow glowing character says to Nolen as it reaches the ground. As its feet touch the sand, smoke arises. "And I let you live with these failures because I knew that The TV could finally be mine when I was ready."

"Please, just list-," Nolen starts. The glowing man reaches an arm out and wraps his fingers around Nolen's face. His screams are muffled as the fingers slowly melt into Nolen's skull, little pieces of meat splatting onto the sand. Nolen's body collapses onto his knees, the man keeping his hand fixed in place. As his fingers meet in the middle of Nolen's head, the man's pointed head turns in our direction. All of the spotlights seem to dim as the light-emitting off of the glowing man grows. I'm the first to swiftly shift to run down the stairs. As I am halfway down the dusty, creaking steps, Nexgas' body tumbles between my stretching legs.

He lands on the bunker's floor, a giant burning handprint torn into his black outfit. I think for a moment he is dead, but I see a twitch in his arms. As I run down the second half, Maya and Heaven's Eye run out of the server area. They crouch down to check Nexgas' vitals, all while I step over some creeping vines.

"He's still alive," Maya quickly says as she puts two fingers all over Nexgas' arms. "Someone get Box Master; we need to leave this place."

"I will," I say, moving down the bunker halls toward the living quarters. "Make sure they don't make it down here before I'm back."

I move past Maya into a hallway, turning right to the sleeping chambers. I pass greenish-yellow wallpaper, buzzing white lights, and chipped brown wooden doors until I reach one labeled 'BM.' I put my hand on the fingerprint-ridden golden doorknob, twisting it to the left. The door creaks open, sounding almost like a muffled scream. I hear a boom from above as the bunker wobbles. I enter the utterly dark room of Box Master, reaching my arms out to the damp walls for a light switch. My fingers touch something protruding from the walls, and the lights jerk on when I pull down on it. Instead of a typical small bedroom, I'm met with the sight of a dark room. Windows on the other side let in small traces of red light, and the walls stretch in each direction endlessly. Rows of tall beige desks with cracked white computer monitors line the space. Every cast shadow appears to darken the more I look around. Silhouetted dark figures lurk in the corners of my eyes.

"Box Master?" I call out. My voice echoes a few times. I turn around to see the door I came through gone, and I face a clean white wall. The red light shines upon it as cracks form. I step back, the desks stopping me in my tracks. The black cracks begin to bleed red, which blends in with the red lighting. I turn back to the windows, which pulse in rhythm with my heart. I grab one of the monitors and throw it at the glass. It shatters, but the shards and monitor freeze in midair after passing the window frame. I quickly jump over a few desks, climbing through the shattered glass. As I pass through, gravity disappears, and my movements are slower and less responsive. I look around at a large green clearing, large oak trees blooming with life, and blue skies. The leaves slowly float around as they break away from the branches. Everything is peaceful until the blue sky darkens into red, and the trees erupt in flames.

My arms and legs are pulled back into the window, with my body bending in half. I try to resist, but I cannot move anything. The once peaceful landscape in front of me crumbles like paper as the stationary shards of glass push me into the office, forming back into the whole window. The red lights reappear and paint the room once more, and all the monitor screens turn to face my floating, bent body. Eyes appear on the screens. Bloodshot white eyes hiding in black shadow.

I begin to shake as an arm grabs onto me from behind. It pulls me past the office through a crack in the bleeding wall. I fly out and hit a familiar concrete wall.

"We've been double-crossed," Maya says as she pulls me up from the ground. "Box Master and Nolen are both working for The Star."

She pulls me along the ground, the rough granite ground scraping my back as she does. I relax as sharp pains in my spine and pelvis pulse around my body. I'm laid next to Nexgas, whose body has been covered in green vines and white daffodils. Maya and Heaven's Eye stand over me as more booms and rocks fall from the ceiling. Cracks form above me as dust flutters down.

"Ok, you gotta get him on your back, and we'll leave through the back entrance," Maya says to Heaven's Eye, who nods as he slides his arms under me. I get a better look at his white and yellow spandex suit and long wrinkled face as he throws me over his shoulder. He runs back the way I just came; the path to Box Master's room. We run by it, and I look at the closed door with an expression of hatred. Heaven's Eye's soft steps and graceful movements leave the trip very comfortable. We reach the end of the hallway, and Maya swipes the moldy wallpaper, which opens the wall up.

It leads to a shining silver elevator with guard railings lining the middle. Heaven's Eye brings me in, pushing me off his shoulder until I slam onto the ground feet first. Then, I pull myself back up with the railings as Maya quickly runs in. Finally, she closes the doors herself by pushing them with her talon-like fingers.

"That should keep them away for a bit," she says. "We need to get to Usnax; maybe someone can help us. I'm sure there's still smugglers and underground trails we can use, right?"

"Don't count on it," Heaven's Eye says. His eyes both shine a soft yellow as the elevator begins to rise. The white light above us buzzes as little flies dance around it. "Jesus, how could we let this happen? I mean, how long have they been part of our group?"

"Fuck it, we should've known it would happen someday," I say. "The prices some people would pay for our heads on their walls."

"Why did TV Man have to leave us?" Maya groans. She rubs her hands against her face as she huffs. "It's like he just gave up on us."

"He has to be somewhere," I say. The elevator stops, the machine jerking us around as the doors slowly open. We're greeted by the dark, deserted sands of the Usnax border, right behind the dune covering the bunker door. I step out of the elevator, looking around to see blasts of light coming from the tanks.

"Come on," Maya says, pushing me forward. We sneak away from the bunker, moving toward the city of Usnax. On the horizon, I can see it. The broken skyline of a once-great city. The tall skyscrapers are now a skeleton of their former glory, with shards of glass barely hanging onto the rebar frames. The small townhouses now just ruined remains, just as the shops and public areas are. The streets are covered in dirty, empty cars, and piles of ash are all that's left of most of the population. The street lights and signs on the sidewalks have already fallen or are hanging on by a thin rope.

The damage is minimal on the city's outskirts, but the destruction is the worst on the inner rings. The cause of the fallout was the gym, located in the heart of the metropolis. One day it lit up, blasting through people and buildings like a knife to butter. Some of us lucky enough to only feel a punch of the blast were left with these unwanted powers. But most perished. They are the lucky ones.

A large circular black concrete fence wraps around the city, protected by barbed wire and now defunct cameras. They used to be patrolled by armed guards, who now bow to Star Man. We easily slip through one of the doors into the city, this one labeled with a red E16 area marking. We start in the outermost region of the city, the least ruined of Usnax. The only damage to cars is the popped tires and shattered glass, and the buildings have minimal cracks. The roads are still infected with potholes and ditches leading to the underground sewer system.

We pass by one or two-story buildings, mostly houses, and stores. Windows and doors are boarded up, and signs hang on by bent nails. Rubble and debris line corners and alleyways. The entire city has a gray and brown color pallet, and the air smells of ash. Smoke from unknown sources still pollutes the clouds, even after thirty-six years.

Eventually, we run into the best place to go in East Usnax, the large building of the Usnax Mall.

~The Duo~

"How long have we been walking for?" Heaven's Eye asks. "Surely, if someone wanted to help us, they would've been here already."

"Hey, look! If anyone would hide somewhere, it would be a mall," Maya says, breaking the depressing mood. Instead, she points to a large, slightly upkept entrance to the East Usnax mall. A large, fluorescent blue arch labeled with a mall logo marks the entry to the parking lot, which is riddled with unkempt vehicles. The main entrance to the mall is a tall gray wall with some sliding glass doors. Due to the explosion, we walk through the frames of the doors as the yellow stained glass covers the brown tiled mall floor.

The inside is barren, besides all of the vegetation. Store entrances are locked with heavy metal gates, a few escalators have fallen to the ground, and ceiling tiles hang down, exposing dark wiring and crawl spaces. Trees in trash bags, empty fountains, and cracked benches remind me of what once was here. We pass by a few more stores, one notable being a candle store with shining green fire endlessly burning inside.

One illuminated sign catches our eyes. An image of a cartoon burger with a red rabbit flashes on and off in what looks to be a pattern.

"Is that morse code?" I ask myself. Heaven's Eye hears me and looks up to the sign. Blink, blink, blink.

Blink. Blink. Blink. Blink, blink, blink. It stays unlit for a moment before repeating.

"That's SOS," Maya points out.

"Yeah, and that can't be a coincidence," I say. We enter a ruined family establishment. Ripped red cushioned seats next to tables holding thirty-six-year-old pizzas, a tattered neon carpet before a closed curtain stage, and some dusty prizes behind a smashed glass counter. Heaven's Eye wipes some dust off the counter, and Maya pokes at the moldy, fly-ridden pizza corpse.

"Hello?" a sharp voice calls out. I look into the dark back of the restaurant. All I can see are a few blue patched-up blankets covering unknown objects. One of the blankets rises and falls to the ground, revealing a man with furry brown skin and cat-like green eyes. His ears also sit closer to the top of his head, and his top lip molds over his mouth.

"Who are you?" I ask. Heaven's Eye and Maya take notice of the man too. He walks into some of the natural light being let in from cracks in the ceiling. A clean purple suit shimmers as it hits the light.

"You first. This is my property. Are you here from The Star? Because I told him I don't HAVE anyone he wants," the cat-human says. Instead, he scrunches his hands into fists, and I hold my arms up.

"Listen, do you have any safe passage for some travelers?" I ask, making sure to choose my words carefully. "We just need to get to the other side of Usnax safely."

"You aren't the only ones," the man says. He points at the other few blanket-covered people, which all reveal themselves. Most are dirty, malnourished humans huddling together for warmth, but one stands out.

One man steps into the light with slicked-back gray hair, a pointed nose, lips of gold, and one green and one purple eye. He wears a black jumpsuit with two purple stripes on either side, a silver belt, and his signature purple fedora.

We have found TV Man.

"Matthew?" I yell out in shock. TV Man raises an eyebrow and turns to the cat man.

"Who are these people?" Matthew asks. I shake my head after hearing it. I reach out, but Matthew takes a step back.

"I am Rowan, and I help people like you cross the underground of Usnax, but we haven't been able to move out. There are patrols in the inner rings," the cat man says. He turns around and ushers the others to get back under their blankets. They all retreat into the back, pulling their covers over themselves and lying around on the ground. Rowan faces us and shrugs his shoulders.

"You could join us, but it would probably be a waste of time," he says.

"I know that one," I say, pointing to where Matthew hid. I attempt to walk toward him, but Rowan steps before me. He holds his hands against my chest and pushes me back.

"They're all really fucked in the head, ok?" he whispers. "I can barely keep them from trying to run away at this point."

"Then we could transport them using the sewers, right?" Maya asks. I turn to my right to see her behind the prize counter. She's holding up a manhole cover and looking down into a small hole that emits a green light. "I think."

"It's too risky. We don't know what could be down there," Rowan complains. Instead, he removes his hands from my chest and walks to the counter. He bends over to look down into the hole. "And why is the water green?"

"It might be our best shot," Heaven's Eye chips in. He jumps over the counter and takes the manhole cover from Maya. "Do we want to try?"

"I can go first to see if it's safe," I say. Rowan awkwardly smiles and nods his head. He glances at the blanketed survivors for a moment while staying silent. After a quick thought, he turns back to me.

"You first, and if there's anything down there, tell us," he says. I give him a quick nod as I climb over the counter. Maya stands up and lets me pass by her. I look down into the green sea of liquid, grabbing onto a silver ladder on the side. I climb down into the tube of splashing sounds and indescribable smells. The arching brown and red walls bend around me, and the sewer trails off in both directions, ending in darkness.

I hop down onto a thin platform, hugging the wall trying not to fall. The smooth, slow flow of the sludgy green liquid splashes around, and I hear whispers from above. I look around the walls, seeing little white plaques of red arrows and unreadable labels.

"I think it's safe!" I yell up to the others. Just as I say that a roar erupts through the area. "Hold on, stay up there!"

"What?" Maya yells down.

"STAY UP THERE FOR A SECOND!" I yell back up. It seems Maya did not hear me because she slides down the ladder, joining my side. "I told you not to come."

"I heard the roar and couldn't miss whatever it came from," Maya says. She walks around the platform less carefully than I do, walking along the edge right above the liquid. "Which way did it come from?"

"Every way," I say. I slide along the platform away from the ladder, trying to move along. "We should find some sort of path or map."

"I'll lead the way," Maya says, moving me out of the way and marching onward. I take a deep breath and move slightly away from the wall, walking quicker through the sewer. Along the way, the path splits into two. The left leads to a staircase leading up, and our side continues into a downward slide. A dam of trash and garbage bags blocks the liquid from flowing down, so Maya quickly jumps down and slides through the darkness.

"Christ," I say as I attempt to follow. My foot is caught on a garbage bag, so I slam face-first into the murky slide and tumble down until I crash into a shallow pool of clear water. Then, I raise my head out of the clean tasting water and see Maya standing before a blue wooden door with a little yellow lightbulb. Straight and bending bronze pipes line the walls, appearing from void-like holes in the ceiling. They drip with clear drops, splashing against raised wall edges.

"There's something behind here," Maya says, wings appearing on her back from thin air. First, a bone-like structure erupts from two holes in the back of her jumpsuit. Then, delicate blue and white feathers grow from them. "I can feel it."

"What are you talking about?" I ask. Maya lays a hand on the door, and the wood crumbles beneath her touch. I stand in awe as the wall opens up to the abandoned tracks of a subway station. "This makes sense. How could you do that?"

"The door…it spoke to me," Maya says. I'm a little freaked out and confused, but I shrug it off. I walk onto the bouncy roach houses that are the subway tracks. Bugs scurry under my feet as I try to move past the pillars that hold up the gray concrete ceiling. I entirely cross the paths, climbing onto the yellow subway platform. I look at the empty dark blue wooden benches, seeing shards of clothing and a turned-over stroller in the far right corner. Broken digital advertisements line the white tile walls, some being wholly broken while I can make out the messages of others.

"Where is the train?" Maya asks, climbing up the platform to join me. She sighs at the sight of the stroller, walking over and pulling it up straight. "Probably couldn't make it past… never mind."

Some security gates lead to a staircase leading up to some natural sunlight in the middle of the wall.

"I think we found our way," I say to Maya. She takes a look up the staircase and nods to me. We both trek back to the slide, looking for a way to climb back up.

"I might be able to fly up," Maya says. She flaps her bony wings, trying to get off the ground. She is unable to lift even her feet out of the water.

"We can look around for a ladder or something," I say. So I turn around to look for something to use as I hear some flapping from behind me. I look to see Maya slowly bringing herself up.

"I still got it," she says to herself. She picks up my shoulders with her feet and carries me to the top of the slide. She tries to drop me onto the platform but accidentally lets go too early. I fall and splash into the green liquid and scream, thinking I will die. Maya lands on the side platforms and laughs as I realize it's just ordinary water. I look down to see the sewer floors are an extended light source that shines green.

"So the water is SAFE?" I scream to myself, swimming to the platform where Maya stands. She snickers as I pull my drenched body out of the river. I look down at my white shirt and red pants, which droop down and add more weight to my walk. Luckily, my curly black hair isn't long enough to block my face. As we walk back to the ladder, my movement being slow and more aggressive, we turn a corner and see Rowan, Matthew, and a few survivors already down here.

"What are you all doing down here already?" Maya asks. Rowan turns around, and we see the look of terror on his face. He points up to the manhole and puts the finger on his mouth.

"They found us," he whispers. I look up at the manhole, seeing a short black and orange light shine through. I push past Rowan, jumping onto the ladder and peeking my eyes through to the restaurant. Then, through a crack in the counter glass, I see a cloud of smoke and Heaven's Eye standing his ground in front of it. The smoke emerges from a body of pure, nude yellow-skinned muscle and the sharpest curves. The body seems to emit a glow as it approaches Heaven's Eye, who tries to throw wet paper plates at it as he backs away.

"Get away from me!" Heaven's Eye yells out. He backs up into a wall, where the buff man grabs onto his throat. We watch as the veiny, pulsing arms of the man struggle to crush Heaven's Eye's throat. He tries to gasp for air, but purple slowly overtakes his skin. He scratches at the man's hands, with skin flaking off and little droplets of blood flying around. All his efforts are futile as the man removes one hand and closes all his fingers except his thumb. He slowly presses it into Heaven's Eye's eyes, the optical orbs popping with yellow sludge squirting onto the man's chiseled face. The man drops Heaven's Eye to the ground, where his gaping eyes stare me down through the counter's glass.

The buff man looks around, flipping over tables and ripping open the cushioned seats. He throws balls of wool around, searching for something or someone. Then, as he walks over to the curtained stage, I look at his oddly square buttocks, which seem to glow blue and red. Then, when he disappears behind the tattered red curtains, I quickly slide down the ladder, accidentally bumping into Matthew.

"Hey!" he quickly shouts out. I apologize and walk over to Maya, who is conversing with Rowan.

"Well, we are down one, but we have a way out," I cut in. Maya looks at me with a bit of annoyance.

"I just told him that," she says with some sass.

"Alright, sorry, but we should go. Now," I say, sliding between the two. I motion with my hand for them to follow me, which nobody does. I turn around. "Let's go."

"They aren't able to move that fast," Rowan says. "We'll need to be slow with them."

I storm up to Rowan, pointing a finger in his face, which makes him back up a step.

"Listen here, if we don't move now, that man up there will kill us all," I yell at him. Rowan's eyelids arch, his pupils widening. I quickly pull my arm down and continue my walk back to the slide. Maya shortly follows, and Rowan ushers the survivors to as well.

As we reach the slide, I let Maya retake the lead, followed by Matthew, the survivors, then Rowan. Before he ventures down, however, he turns to me.

"I'm helping you to a secure safe house, and that's it. Then you get the fuck out of my face," he says before pushing himself down the slide.

"I'm sorry that I don't want to die due to slowness," I whisper to myself. I take one last look into the darkness of the green sewer before tripping again down into the little puddle of water. I join the others on the subway platform as Maya stares into one of the tunnels from the edge. "You ok?"

"Yeah, I'm just wondering where the corpses of the trains are," she says. I shrug and walk through the security gates onto the studded stairs up to the surface. It leads to the middle of a large park with leafless black trees, a dirt ditch that's probably a dried-up lake, and winding silver cobblestone paths. Tall light poles flicker with flashes of yellow light as plants and vines overtake them. Rowan stands at the edge of the ditch, looking down into the brown pit.

"I got you a map," he says, handing me a folded piece of paper. I take it and unfold it into a large map of winding lines and large blobs of blue color. White words of streets, buildings, and areas cover the dark and light blue outlines. Large bold letters spell out 'East Usnax' over the entire map. "We need to go here, just a few blocks away."

He points to a giant dark blue blob in the bottom left corner. A label reads 'Globe Robustness.' He points to another blob, this one light blue, around the middle. The title reads 'Magonish National Park.'

"We are here," he says. "That gym is the safehouse. I usually drop people off to a Stephen Ramos. He can get you safe travel across the globe or even off-planet."

"There's off-planet travel?" I ask loudly. Rowan looks around and shushes me.

"They can't go off-planet," he says, pointing to the survivors laying down on termite-eaten benches. "There's something about Matthew that I don't quite understand."

"Yeah, he used to be part of our group," I tell Rowan. "He was trying to kill Star Man. He knew about the army, so he was trying to build his own with the failures of Star Man's tests."

"So what, he's actually from off-world?" Rowan asks. I nod my head. "So why is he acting like this?"

"He's not himself, and I don't know why," I say, looking at Matthew. I can see him sleeping in a patch of overgrown emerald grass on the ground. "But at this point, the battle is over, and we lost."

"I'm sorry to hear that. But my father used to tell me that no matter what, in the end, nobody ever wins. All we can really do is rest and forgive each other," Rowan says. "Alright, enough standing around. Let's get going."

I fold the map back up and shove it into my back pocket. We walk over to Maya, who stands watching the survivors sleep. I motion my head, and she nods. We wake up the survivors, ensuring they are fully awake before we begin the next journey.

I occasionally check the map as we traverse the increasingly worse roads. As we venture into the heart of Usnax, the buildings become increasingly abandoned and destroyed, with the streets completely covered in ash, rocks, and debris. We have to almost climb the wreckage to reach the gym. The sight of it is chilling, with black ash covering one lone wall in a crater of silhouettes of the dead. The black-covered yellow wall stands alone on a hill of rocks, looking like an island in an empty sea.

We climb onto the island of ruin, seeing the gray dust-covered equipment and benches. Rowan walks over to the lone wall, where two large black doors angle out from the floor. He opens both, one at a time, and motions for the survivors to walk down.

"Stephen is just down there. He will help you. Good luck," Rowan says to Maya and me. I attempt to ask him to stay for a moment until I hear a crash from below. I quickly run into a damp, gray underground area with desks and screens lining the place. I come to a screeching halt as I see a bald man with forward-pointing nostrils and a small mouth wearing a bright yellow jumpsuit staring at Matthew. A smashed white and blue vase and some decomposing red flowers are at his feet.

"TV Man?" the man asks. "Where have you been?"

Matthew isn't phased and seems to not know the man is asking him a question.

"What happened to our army? How could you let Star Man take them?" the man begins to yell. He gets into Matthew's face, who backs up and starts to whimper. Rowan runs down behind me and tackles the man to the ground, slapping him in the face.

"Stephen! What did I say about them?" Rowan yells out, his voice cracking a few screens. "Over the PHONE?"

"I know him! I worked with that one!" Stephen yells out, pointing to Matthew with one hand and covering a bloody nose with the other. We all turn to Matthew, huddled up in his blue blanket on the ground, hiding from everyone. "I know you won't believe me, but look!"

Stephen removes something from a pocket with very shaky hands, putting it up to Rowan's face. He takes it and turns around to face us. It's a piece of wrinkled white paper with a photo on it. Rowan looks at it, and his eyes widen. He slowly turns it around so Maya and I can see it. The picture is of Matthew in a purple fedora just like

Rowan's and a seemingly endless army of featureless beings behind him.

Matthew walks over and looks at it, and a streak of green and purple rises through his body. His eyes go blank with purple color as he quickly throws the blanket to the side and snatches the fedora from Rowan's head.

"Hey!" Rowan yells out. He tries to grab it back, but Matthew swiftly slams it onto his own head. A few more pulses of green and purple glissade until he falls to the ground. Rowan catches him and slowly lays him on the cold floor. Finally, I look up at the screens lining the far wall, each showing a different view of the outside.

"Who are you?" I ask Stephen, who stands up and wipes his nose. He sniffs some blood back up, and I see a small, shriveled brown orb fall out of his left nostril.

"I was someone, like you, hiding from the star lord. Then, this man found me a few years ago and told me about some army. Then he kind of went a little crazy and disappeared," Stephen explains.

"When did he appear?" I ask. Stephen shrugs.

"Maybe ten years ago?" he guesses.

"That's when he disappeared from us…," I say, my words trailing off as I turn to Matthew. Something about him seems off to me. "That photo sparked something in him. Maybe we can do that again?"

"I don't have much, but I have some files and documents from our army," Stephen says. So I pause him by holding out a hand.

"Wait, tell me about that army," I say.

"Well, he told me he was here because The Star is plotting to become the ruler of the universe? Or something," Stephen explains. "He thought The Star was building an army, so we made one out of energy solutions and corpses. After he disappeared from ME, the army was unsuccessful in taking over the headquarters of The Star, so they were all taken. I have since resorted to what I do now. Smuggling people away."

"You know where The Star is?" I ask first. Stephen nods. "Any way you could get us there?"

"Listen, pal, you're better off just leaving Earth now," Stephen says, shaking his head. "Nothing left for any of us here."

"Here's what we'll do, Stephen," I say, marching over to him. "You let them leave, and we'll get Matthew his identity back."

I point first to the survivors, then to Maya, Rowan, and Matthew. I also point right in Stephen's face. Stephen stands towering over me with a blank expression as he sighs. He walks over to a random computer and clicks some of the keyboard buttons.

"Jeez, you really are bossy," Rowan says, walking over to me.

"I know he is the key to killing The Star. TV Man is still somewhere in there," I say, looking at Matthew again.

"Goddammit!" Stephen yells out from his computer. I walk over to see the screen flashing with an image of a gray cartoon gorilla beating his chest. The words 'FUTILE' flash in big, bold red letters at the bottom.

"What's going on?" Rowan asks, walking over to us. All of the screens in the room suddenly switch to the image, each slightly delayed than the last. On the screens on the wall, a silhouette of the gorilla's head appears, creating a looming shadow over the cartoons.

"I am the Phantom Guerilla, and I have been sent by our Lord, The Almighty Star, to send a message."

"What's the message?" Maya calls out.

"TV Man will NOT succeed, and his fall from grace will be studied forever."

~The Stash~

"Christ, this piece of shit," Stephen says. He runs over to one of the computers in the right corner of the room, the only screen without the gorilla's presence. Rowan turns to the survivors and helps them back up the stairs. Maya stands by my side, looking up at the oversized shadow face. The dancing gorilla animation ceases, and the background switches to an aerial view outside the gym. I can see Rowan and the others moving across the rocks, attempting to hide under some loose boulders.

"Can we get someone outside to see what's watching us?" Stephen yells as he types away at a keyboard. I run up the stairs to the surface, where I see nothing in the sky. I look around, confused. The sound of helicopter blades cuts through the air, but still, nothing appears.

"Are you ok?" Rowan asks from my side. I look over to see Rowan comforting Matthew specifically, instead of all the survivors.

"Yeah," I respond. "I thought I heard something."

As I turn to walk back to the basement, Matthew speaks up.

"The Phantom can't be seen by light," he says. I slowly look at him, seeing his eyes pulsing with purple. I walk over.

"Excuse me?" I ask; Rowan holds out an arm.

"He's been through trauma; give him a break," Rowan says. I nod and walk back to the basement doors. Before descending, I look back at the sky, where a gleam appears across the shadow of a towering building in the distance. I ignore it and return to Stephen, who's finally gotten the screens to display the standard views. He wipes sweat off his brow, brushing his sweaty arms on his yellow suit.

"I got him off, but who's telling how long until he's back," Stephen says. "We should get back to getting Matt's memories back, eh?"

"How will we do that?" I ask.

"We need to find his secret stash. I think I know where it is, but it's a far away spot. On the outskirts of Eastern Usnax, basically," Stephen responds. So I pull out my map and unfold it, giving it to him. He points to a small area in the top left. "One of these buildings has some photos and documents."

"You don't know which one?" Maya asks. Stephen sorrowfully shakes his head.

"Unfortunately, no, but we can all go together. We must leave the others here. Just us three," Stephen says, a small smile creeping upon his face. I look at Maya, who looks at me, and we all begin nodding. "Ok, good, we agree. The first order of business is to get there. There's no direct underground route, so we must travel above ground."

"Is it safe?" I ask. Stephen hesitates for a moment and pats me on my shoulder.

"Nowhere is."

He passes between Maya and me, up the stairs and out of view. I quickly glance at Maya, who shakes her head. I walk up to the surface, which is now cloudy, and rumbles can be heard all around. The sunlight is now gone, and I notice the building's shadow from before. It's still the same darkness as when the sun was out, which I keep in mind. I see Stephen stepping over the rubble, taking significant steps.

—

First, we reach the same park as before, with the giant ditch. The twisted black trees seem taller than before. Far away, I can see figures marching through the burned streets, with spotlights shining. I pay no attention. The buildings now progress backward than when I entered. Now, they grow more and more fixed and look more lively. The gray and brown tones of the ruins in the center of Usnax now make room for occasional bright colors hidden under dirt tracks.

Drop.

Was that water? Another drop hits the ground in front of me; a splash erupts from the cobblestone path I walk upon. The rain starts slowly, only hitting my skin a few times a minute. I can see every tiny droplet as it falls. The clouds grow darker like more are combining.

Drop. Drop.

The rain picks up, falling faster in front of me. It washes away dust and dirt off the environment and me; thunder claps while lightning strikes. We leave the park, making it to the mall again. We enter through a different entryway leading right to a food court. Abandoned steel tables and large plants, broken ceiling tiles, and shattered store signs. Mice run around, avoiding us as we walk through. Food sits on top of the tables, left alone for years and only touched by the embrace of mold. We can hear the sound of the rain tap against the ceiling as we walk through.

—

We exit the mall, still no one says a word. As we pass into the outermost area of Eastern Usnax, a white light appears from between two bulky red towers. Both are intact, with the only damage being shattered glass. The light forms into a figure, and we stop before it. The figure becomes a skeleton with yellow bones and a tattered brown cloak.

"Is he with you?" it asks in a very echoey voice.

"Who?" I ask.

"You must tell The TV that it is over."

"Excuse me?" I ask again. "Why don't you tell him yourself?"

"I cannot track him to an exact location... I'm lucky enough to have found you," the skeleton says. He holds out a bony hand, which has been split in half. "Please. He needs to realize. It's over."

"Why do you want him?" Maya asks. Before the skeleton can respond, it shines back into the light, which disappears. "Then let us continue walking…and we can tell him later."

"Should we?" I ask.

"Let's just keep going," Stephen says, not acknowledging the skeleton's message.

—

The rest of the journey is the same. Passing by sad reminders of a life lost to a mad God. The houses that used to be housed by families of humans now hold families of infestations. The streets lay silent, not bustling with the sounds of cars gone for years. Even the wind struggles to be heard. All that's left is the fire and smoke of a date long remembered.

Nobody even knows how the rest of the world is doing. We know they were overrun as well, shortly after Usnax was. The president lost his campaign to Star Man eight years after the bombing due to a hacked vote. All communications to other nations were cut shortly after, as were all transportation. I had family across the waters. I doubt they're alive anymore. Probably floating around a river in a trash bag somewhere. I hate the thought, but it's probably true.

I used to think that together anything is possible. Now I know that together, your odds of dying are higher. To think that in this large-scale universe, nobody thought to try to save us. We're just left to fend for ourselves as Earth is used for some unknown battleground. I hate it.

"We're here," Stephen says. I stop thinking and pay attention to the large, off-white three-story building in front of us. It has a triangular roof, stretching up into a red brick chimney. Windows adorn the front and are all intact. A tall metal fence guards the perimeter, but the entry gates are open for us to walk through. The courtyard looks beautiful, having large patches of flowers decorating the benches, entrance archways, and the outline of the building.

"The Eastern Usnax Psychiatric Hospital," Stephen says. "I... didn't want to come back here."

"It looks nice...and kept well decorated," I say. Stephen stops in front of the entrance glass doors and turns to me.

"Please just...," he pauses for a second. "I had a bad encounter here a few years back."

Stephen turns back around and pushes through the doors into the main lobby, a pristine white room with pillars covered in inspirational quotes and blocky brightly colored chairs on either side. In the far-middle, a reception desk rests before a dark, black metal door with a red wheel valve. The entire place smells of hand sanitizer, and the white light adds to the cleanliness. We walk across the glossy, beige hardwood floor to the desk, which holds neatly stacked and organized papers. Stephen walks around it, back to the door, and slowly turns the valve to the right. It's stuck at first, and he has to push it with both hands and his chest. Then, it cracks to the right, where he can easily continue spinning it around.

I can hear the sounds of clacking metal and churning gears as the door shakes and dust falls off. Stephen pulls on the valve, and we're met with a dark hallway.

"After you," he says, pointing to me. I look at the hallway, then to Stephen, then back to the beckoning darkness. I swallow my doubts, walking past the desk and past Stephen, who guides me in with his arm. I walk into the void, all the sounds, smells, and my whole sense of anything being vaporized.

Crying.

Crying?

I hear crying from behind. Who could be crying now? Maya?

I look back, expecting to see the white lobby. I'm only met with a smaller, dirtier room. The four walls I find myself trapped in are a light blue on the bottom and beige on the top. Smears of feces and dirt smudge across them. A lone barred window shines in light, but it's so high up and thin that I can't see out of it. The floor is home to actual dirt and a stained mattress bent out of shape. The white fabric is now dotted with yellow, brown, and dark red circles.

I turn back around to be met with a chamber of cells. I expect them to rattle with inhabitants, but they all stay silent. A horrid smell, however, grows as I move closer to the middle of the arena. I look at all of the enclosures, seeing…humans. I walk up to one, seeing a bare woman lying on the ground, a brown paper bag on her head and a broken glass bottle spotted in blood in her left hand. Red streaks line her inner thighs. I raise my hand to my mouth, vomit rising in my throat. The sound of laughter erupts as suddenly two men appear from behind me. They walk up to the bars, laughing as they shine black flashlights onto her body. They both wear beige shirts tucked into light blue dress pants and brown shoes. Their faces I can't make out, but their intentions I can.

I move onto another cell, looking in to see a man wearing simple gray clothes, but his body is almost skeletal. He sits with his legs up to his chest on another stained mattress, next to a shattered white sink. His head shakes violently as he turns his head to me. I see his face, drooping eyelids with a hopeless look in his eyes.

I'm pulled back, falling to the ground and splashing through a sea of water. I quickly sit up, appearing to be in some makeshift bathtub. It seems to be made of a broken fridge, the lightbulb between my bare feet. I roll out of the side onto a cracked tile floor. I'm pulled up by a woman, similar to the one I just saw. She's also unclad, and nail slashes run across her chest. Her breast area is flat, with large stitch circles running around where the nipples should be. The deep cuts across her body end around her neck…and start above her vulva. The area is freshly shaved, but I can see little bumps and sores, most likely the reason for the frantic itching. I look at her face, seeing a beautiful woman with long black hair.

Who are these people?

I stand up, and the woman begins pleading for me to help. I try to put my hands on her shoulders to calm her down, but I can't move them. I see barbed wire wrapped around my wrists, binding them together. The barbs cut into my skin, and I can feel the boiling pain run through me.

"I want to help; I don't know where I am!" I yell out. The woman jumps at my outbreak, and her face begins to shake. I can see her emerald eyes water and tears stream down her cheeks. She doesn't break down, which makes it more uncomfortable to watch her stare at me while crying. "I'm sorry!"

The woman's eyes drop down an inch, and they look to not be focused on anything. It seems like she's out of it. She turns around and wobbles out of a sudden doorway in the beige and blue walls. Blood drips from her body, leaving little prints behind her. I try again to pull my arms apart, but it causes the barbs to dig deeper into my skin. I look around the bathroom to see my reflection in a cracked mirror above the fridge tub. My face is the one of Stephen's, and my clothes are his bright yellow jumpsuit. I try to yell out, but my voice doesn't come out. I try again, but all that happens is a quiet, poof noise.

"She's dead?" I hear from behind. The bathroom has now morphed into a dark space where only two men stand. It's the two from the chamber.

"Found her in the West wing," the second man says, with no sense of remorse. "Thankfully…."

I take a deep breath to prepare myself.

"She only got her excrement and STDs over some stalls and a few of the women in the Lesser Treatment area," he finishes. They both pause for a moment and laugh.

"Less of a job for the janitor, thank God. He'd be PISSED if he had to clean more than two rooms again," the first man jokes. "He made me clean up some shit on the corpse last week. I mean, it wasn't a lot, but he could've done his job."

The two men laugh once more; this time, it turns into howling. The volume becomes too much to bear until I shut my eyes and cover my ears. As soon as I notice my arms are free, I try to open my eyes. They won't budge. I touch around my eyelids, feeling some delicate stitches. I try to scream, but my mouth won't shift. I can feel my brain spin around in my head as liquid leaks from my ear canal. It flows down my cheeks, seeping through the open edges of my lips. It covers my tongue, and a bitter, chocolate-like flavor fills my mouth. I try to swallow it just to get rid of the taste, but it doesn't move. The liquid then fills my throat, and my breathing skips a beat.

I begin suffocating, my ears never stopping and the river never-ending. It all feels as though it goes on forever until my eyes burst open. A garish light is put into my eyes. Colors of green, yellow, and red dance around my head.

"He's awake, Jesus fuck…," Stephen curses. He removes the light, and I see him and Maya sweating profusely. They stand above me as I lay on something soft. My head still spins from the trippy encounter. "Listen, boy, you can't let him get into your head."

"Huh?" I ask. Their voices sound slightly muffled, and my vision is somewhat blurry. Stephen angrily shakes his head and whispers something to Maya.

"We found the Goddamn files," he says, holding up a few beefy manilla folders. Maya takes them from him, handing-off a round purple orb. "Eat this; you should feel better in a bit."

He hands it to me, and I shakingly take it, and I try to put it in my mouth. I fail, and I just kind of rub it against my lips until it bumps into one of my teeth. I slowly bite a piece off, and the bumpy, vinegary skin contrasts the sweet, smooth inside. I swallow a portion, and I feel the spinning slow, and I can see more clearly. I'm still in the lobby, lying down on the desk. The papers are now all over the ground, and the valve door is shut.

"What happened to me?" I ask.

"Same thing that happened to me," Stephen says. "I came here a few years ago to retrieve these documents when…I went through a similar vision. This place used to be open during the beginning of the supers rise. The government, at the time, funded it so anyone that believed they had powers could be sent here and 'nurtured.' I remember seeing the articles in two-thousand and three…all of the lawsuits and court cases."

"So do I," Maya says, her eyes darting away from us. "My mother was admitted here…right as the rise was happening. She had BPD, it was like she didn't even know who she was. But they ignored it and grouped her with the misunderstood. She was put in the East wing and…."

"If you don't mind me asking, what happened?" I ask. Maya looks at me, tears in her eyes and across her face. Her beak trembles.

"She was raped."

I don't say a word, Maya looks away from us again.

"Not just by her female cellmate but…by the male and female guards as well. It was a daily occurrence in those wings. You could hear the screaming from outside the building…in the streets. If I didn't run away I…I would've been put in there too."

We let Maya have a moment of grief and dump the trauma on us. She covers her beak with her hands, and her eyes close. Stephen catches her as she falls to her knees, weeping as the rain outside picks up. He looks up at me, and we both stay silent.

~The Elder~

Rowan spots me first.

He stands in the rain, his fur and purple suit soaked. The survivors are all in the basement, huddled together under their blankets. The screens are all shut off to keep the room dark. Maya sits on the bottom step, being there in case they wake up. I stand with Rowan and Stephen under a piece of flooring sticking out from the lone gym wall. We move a boulder over to set the papers out on. They're spread out in three piles; photos, text documents, and scribbles. The images show Matthew with more muscles and a much younger face. He stands proud of Stephen amongst the large army.

Most of the text documents are daily reports. Sightings on the cameras, bird watchers, and weather changes. The scribbles are unintelligible drawings, indecipherable scrawlings of an Alzheimer's victim. We prepare to show Matthew some of these, organizing them into the most vague to too direct. He's brought up by Maya, who holds onto his arms as he stumbles up the stairs.

"Ok, Matthew, what does this photo say to you?" Stephen asks, holding up a monochrome photo of Matthew burning a yellow star sticker with a blocky lighter.

"Star...bad?" he guesses, shrugging ever so slightly.

"This won't go anywhere," Rowan complains, angrily storming off. Stephen tries to show Matthew more photos, but he remains confused about each one. After a while, I leave them and walk down to Maya. Then, I take a seat on the bottom step next to her, where she meddles with her fingernails.

"Are you doing ok?" I ask. She nods. "Why did you go in with us?"

"I hoped we could avoid certain sections of the place. It was hard to keep everything to myself...I elected to stay behind with you while Stephen went for the files because I couldn't bear to go farther," she says, her voice shaking and her eyes still watery. "The government-funded the place, so they had enough money to dodge everything. The place only closed when the owner died from an unknown cause, and his illegitimate son took the money and ran."

"The government continued to fund it even after learning everything? Were all the accusations somehow brushed under the carpet?" I ask.

"Well, there's nowhere else for them to go. If they closed the mental hospital, normal doctors couldn't handle them even if they tried," Maya responds. Rowan walks down the stairs past us, over to the survivors. He sits next to them, whispering to the lot. "Speaking of nowhere to go...someone found out I was unusual, so they alerted the local authorities. They stormed my apartment building, but

I could fly out. I did and didn't look back as I just left into the desert. That was the last time I flew until recently."

"And how did it feel when you regained your flight?"

Maya looks at me with shiny, trembling eyes. A slight smile appears on her face.

"I felt free, just as I did back then," she says.

"We got something!" Stephen yells, running down the stairs with his arms swinging wildly around. He stops above us, his eyes circled with heavy purple bags. "He gave us an address after I showed him this."

He pulls out a photo of the gorilla screen from earlier and must have printed it out.

"Well, what's the address?" Rowan asks, walking toward us from the survivors. A large grin forms on his face.

"1933 Evesham Street, West Usnax. It's a bit of a walk, but it's something," Stephen says. "Rowan, this is where we have to split up. I have someone coming to pick those guys up."

He points to the survivors, huddled up under their blanket, sleeping on each other. Rowan takes a look at them, pondering something. He fiddles with a few loose hairs on his chin.

"Ok," he finally says, turning back around. "I'm keeping Matthew, however."

"You do you, pal. I get bank no matter how many I give," Stephen says. And with that, we all part our ways.

Rowan, Matthew, Maya, and I begin walking West using my map. Stephen stays behind with the rest. Before we split, we say our goodbyes. I'm first, and I give Stephen a stern handshake. He oddly pats me on my hip with his free hand. Maya and Rowan are next, giving him a quick, friendly hug. The last thing we say to him is our farewells.

—

West Usnax is a new sight. Its elevation is lower than Eastern Usnax, and it sits right next to a dam that borders the Arctic Ocean. However, due to the decay and mishandling of the dam over the years, cracks have formed, seeping ocean water through. Most of the Western part is flooded, with only the top of skyscrapers and bridges between them left above. Moss, vines, and roped-up corpses hang from the edges of the bridges, only inches above the sea.

Most West Usnax streets angle down, hence the lower elevation, but a small area of land remains above the water. It's around the middle of the Western front and home to plenty of relaxing townhouses. They sit surrounded by a large building, bordered by a steep declining edge, into the flooded streets below. A makeshift wooden bridge connects the East Usnax slums to the West Usnax residential district.

It shakes as we walk upon it, swaying side to side above the splashing of waves. The clouds continue to pour down rain, the first time I've seen it since before the dark times. The drops drip against the rope handrails that we pull ourselves on. The journey is slow, but we make it over the mile-long bridge onto the overgrown roads of the neighborhoods.

Like the ones in the park, black twisted trees contort around the shells of houses. Exteriors with smashed windows, shredded walls and doors, roofs caved in with saplings growing from within. Mailboxes torn from their posts, cars left to rot on driveways, an authentic ghost town. The numbers on the sides of houses hang from loose rusty nails, and most have fallen.

Luckily, our house is the most intact of the rest.

A two-story Victorian-style house. The walls were light blue but now are a dirtier turquoise. The corners and edges of the house are dark brown, with small termite bites taken out of them. Chipped white shutters bang on the windows, barred up from the inside. A barren chimney lies smokeless on the top of the gray roof, a reminder of gone occupants.

We trudge up the white front stairs to the porch, where a single wooden rocking chair slowly moves. Back and forth, back and forth. The front door is already open like the house is inviting us inside. Then, right through the door, a foreboding staircase rises into the darkness. On the right side, a smoldering living area burns indefinitely. A large flat-screen TV in the far back shimmers with glimpses of a motion picture, and a shattered door hangs on its hinges next to it.

"So, what's so special about this house?" Rowan asks. Matthew walks in behind him, and the purple eyes appear again. He reacts violently, his body thrashing around as his limbs snap around. He falls to the ground, his body being inhumanly contorted.

"The basement... don't...go... it's his trap...," Matthew yells out, his voice shattering glass around us. We all cover our ears as his neck begins bleeding on the front. "It is already over...he will rise soon."

After a loud screech, his body loosens and returns to normal. Tears stream down his cheeks and the blood around his neck is wiped off by Rowan, who holds Matthew in his arms.

"What are you?" he calls out. "Please tell me this isn't my purgatory!"

"Rowan!" Maya yells out. Rowan snaps up at her. His eyes let out a small tear of blood as his mouth trembles. "Pull yourself together! We need to find what's in here."

"I guess I'll check the basement. There's gotta be something there...something he doesn't want us to see," I say. Rowan and Maya look at each other for a moment. Rowan stands up, carrying Matthew across his shoulders.

"I'll be here, and Maya can look on the top floor," Rowan says. Maya rolls her eyes as she walks up the dark, creaking stairs. The handrail cracks and falls down as she walks up and stumbles onto the steps. I see the edge of one fracture her jaw, and a few drops of blood fall out. She curses and gets back up. I nod at Rowan as I walk into the smokey living room. I pass by a mangled couch as I see something under it. A small split in the hardwood floor lets in some unnatural yellow light, so I push the warm couch out of the way. Underneath is a circular brown and red tapestry nailed to the floor in each corner. Luckily, the nails are almost pulled out of the wood, so I lightly tap on them, and they fall over.

I kick the tapestry away, and a small metal trapdoor is revealed. I pull on a small handle on its left side, and it uncovers a ladder leading into a brightly lit corridor. I jump down, skipping the ladder, and bruising my left foot. I land on some prismarine bricks, surrounded by similarly colored walls. Torches sticking from the wall line my way, and I see a few feet in front of me a pile of rocks blocking the path. I walk up to it, trying to dig a way through. For a moment, I see a child's arm reach out, and it causes me to fall backward. I hit my head on the ground, and my eyes close for a moment.

When I recuperate, I look back at the pile to see no arm. I stand and attempt to move the rocks, but they become too heavy to pull. I huff and give up, swinging around to walk back to the ladder. Before I reach it, dull, robotic noises drone around me. The walls crack open, and a blue light emerges in front of me. A rectangular shape forms from the ground, blue streaks of light blasting around me. Some sort of gateway awaits me, and the translucent blue and purple mixture of colors intrigues me.

I feel myself walking toward it, a sound whispering from beyond it.

My hand reaches into the light, and something grabs me from the other end. I snap back into reality and try to pull myself back, but their grip is too much. It drags me into the light, and I fall to the ground, my vision overtaken by the brightness. The colors swim and melt all around me as I hear a familiar voice call my name.

~The Problem~

"Honey?"

"Yes?" I ask in response. I wipe my eyes of the sleep in the corners as I stand up from my bed. I grudgingly walk in just a pair of boxers to the bathroom connected to our bedroom. The purple light from outside is struck as I flip on the yellow light in the bathroom. I see my wife sitting on the silver toilet, wearing a plaid red tank top and pink shorts. She has one hand over her mouth and the other holding a small white stick. Her long blonde hair blocks the view of her face.

"What's that?" I ask, leaning over next to the crusty sink. I brush her hair back with my furry hands to see tears streaming from her face. I stand shocked for a moment, not knowing what is going on. She removes the hand from her mouth, showing off a large-toothed smile. My expression turns to match hers as I look down at the stick to see two tiny red lines. I wrap my arms around her, and we both cry happy tears in unison.

"We did it," she says. Everything changes as I find myself standing in the bathroom doorway, looking into the purple bedroom. The singular large bed is the only thing in my focus as I watch her holding both hands over her mouth. Her blonde hair is now browner, and her stomach is almost the size of a pumpkin. I lean against the unlit bathroom door frame, keeping myself from shedding a tear. We both stay silent as I pull out a brick-like phone to dial our doctor. She picks up.

"Hello?" I hear her soft voice say from the other end.

"They're gone."

I blink and find myself sitting in a small office room, across a desk from the doctor. Her face blanks in my mind, and all I can see is her chapped lips. The space around me also doesn't matter; I can only think about the paper I stare at.

Miscarriage, October 12th, 1999.

I can't even believe it. Anything. My son, Matthew Eese...gone. My wife's in shock and currently in a hospital. I'm stuck with filling out paperwork. Paperwork for premature death. I pick up a dark blue pen beside the slip, signing my name at the bottom. The paper erupts and wraps around my body, spinning me around until I can see her face on the hospital bed. I hold her hand, hearing the beeps of the heartbeat monitor.

A calendar beside her head has a small photo of a smiling cat hanging on a tree, hang in there!

December 12th, 1999.

I hold my wife's hand for the last time. She passes away right next to me, two months after we lost our son. Our child. I can remember the warmth of her fingers on mine fading away as the beeps grew into a drone. The doctors said it was the miscarriage that killed her. It should've been me, right?

The next thing I know, I'm wandering the smoke-covered ruins of a building. I hear screaming, and I dig through the wreckage to find anyone. I only find one person. A small girl, about eight years old. She's almost engulfed underneath rocks. I try to get her out, reaching out to her to grab on. We interlock arms, and I begin to pull her out, but a firefighter pushes me aside, and the link is broken. He attempts to lift the rocks with a fire ax, but his sweaty hands slip, and the rocks collapse.

I could've saved her.

He turns to me, and I see myself reflected in his face shield. I see a broken man with ash and soot painted over my fur. The firefighter tries to calm me down, but I can only think about the girl. I should have stood my ground.

The firefighter yells at me again, and I snap into a clean room. White pillars and walls give a sense of loneliness. I sit on an uncomfortable wooden chair, awaiting someone. A snoring woman with long black hair sits next to me, a snot bubble in rhythm with her breathing. All of the details are fuzzy...I can barely remember anything. I hear a woman's voice, and I'm brought through a steel door into a hallway of absolute difference then the lobby. Blue and beige walls, streaking with questionable things.

As I'm brought into the back of the building, I pass by a slightly open door. I slowly walk past, looking through the crack into a room where two men beat down a bare stringy man with black batons. His screams make it out to the hall but are silenced as the doctor closes it on me. She urges me to continue, and I hesitantly do.

I'm diagnosed with post-traumatic stress disorder that day. Of what specifically?

Everything.

The mall is my following location, where I watch as it becomes more desolate daily. Less and fewer crowds until the day when it closes down.

April 7th, 2025.

Only a few days until I began my path

April 13th, 2025.

I walk the baron stores, seeing signs of life. Fresh crumbs and footprints. An animal? Perhaps. I follow them into a burger shop, where something is writhing around behind red curtains. I pull them out of the way, seeing a man in rainbow spandex hunched over, gnawing on the body of a sewer rat. I could tell he was on the run from something. I gather more rats for him, leading him along with the ruins of Usnax until we stumble across the gym once more. I pause at the sight of the rock pile.

I dig it up, finding the girl's bones and torn pink dress. I take them out and bury them under some dirt a few feet away. I stick a burned plank of wood under the rocks to keep the hole open forever. And as I lead the man along, I meet Stephen, who tells me he smuggles people away.

I leave the man on his way and finally feel like I saved someone. I return to the restaurant, finding someone else. The cycle of saving speeds up until I find Matthew. I see him hiding underneath one of the booth tables. At first, I treated him like any other person I come across. Until I see a small nametag on a blue blanket he holds.

Matthew.

I hug him. I'm reminded of what could have been. I promise to keep him safe and not to leave his side. In respect for....

I keep him around for two years. I smuggle more to Stephen, but Matthew never goes. I can't let him. Then, one day I'm waiting for a wave of patrols to go along as a group of outsides walk in.

"Hello?" my sharp voice calls out.

"Hello, Rowan," a sharper voice says from all around. I slowly open my eyes, two large burly brutes standing before me. Their manhood proves difficult to not be distracted by. I pull my arms down, feeling chains wrapped around my wrists. Blood pools around my lip. My head hangs down, and I see a puddle of sweat and blood beneath my bare hanging body. The orange room around me smells of armpits and morning breath.

"What...do you want?" I struggle to say. A brown wooden door creaks open between the men. They walk out as a short figure strolls in. First, I notice his lack of a jaw. Blood and tissue hang down below tears in his cheeks and nose. His deep black eyes go well with his dark hair, and his outfit is similar to Harvey's; red pants and a white shirt.

The man walks up to me, examining my face. His black eyes move around like dog's. Flaps of skin dance around his neck as he moves around the room like a frantic child. After a few minutes of constant movement, he nods to himself and pulls a key out of his pocket. He sticks it in the chains around my wrists and unlocks them. I drop to the floor, hitting my elbows against the ground. The man throws the key onto my head and walks out. Finally, I push my beaten body up to my feet, rubbing against the wall for support.

I push myself through the door, out into a semi-flooded tube-shaped hallway. Tiny light bulbs shine down every few feet, illuminating the mossy gray brick walls. Dirty green liquid flows around my knees, and I trudge through, looking for traces of the mouthless man. No footprints, handprints, or even signs of life can be found anywhere. I continue to tramp along.

Eventually, my body begins to give. I feel pain across my legs, and my heart beats quicker. My breathing deepens, and it becomes harder to move. I feel like I'm about to fall until I feel the water lower. I feel a little better after. It all sinks into little grates in the ground, which I step over as roaches climb through them. I attempt to control my breathing, which helps a little. My arms wobble at my sides, and my right brushes against something in my pocket.

I quickly pull it out to see a small black flip phone in my hand.

"Where did this come from?" I ask myself. I flip it open, and it flashes on. The brightly lit screen is only populated by one single word; Stephen. I click the 'OK' button, and it begins to dial Stephen. He quickly picks up, and I put the phone to my ear.

"Stephen?" I ask.

"Where the hell are you guys?" he yells from the other line.

"We got transported to his liar... I'm trying to find the others and escape."

"Forget them, just go!" Stephen yells. "It's a death trap for you now!"

"I... can't leave them. Just if you can come, please do. We need another set of hands." I say nothing more, and I flip it closed. I let the phone slip from my fingers onto the ground, leaving it behind as I continue.

—

The tube shortly ends with a staircase. As all sewer-like systems do. I put my hand onto the shaky metal wire handrail, slowly stepping on each loose gray wooden stair. It's not a very long trip, only a dozen stairs onto the next floor, where I walk through a small red and blue striped door at the top into a giant arena area. Tall silver bleachers decorate the walls, and the floor is covered in sand. An ample circular red light shines on a man standing in the middle.

A man in a black suit and a mask, a mask with a large red nose, an elongated smile, and purple hair stands in an upright position, with his hands behind his back.

"Hello, Rowan. I am Sugar Pass. One of a few highly trained soldiers you will come across. I am delighted I am the first you will fight," he says. His voice is high-pitched and squeaky. He puts one leg backward and raises his hands in a battle stance. Before I can react, a projectile is shot past my right arm, which hits Sugar Pass.

He lowers his head to see a raisin lodged in his body armor. He watches as another one blasts into his left leg. He looks up to his left, where a third raisin shoots through his left eye. Sugar Pass doesn't move a muscle as blood starts to flow out of his new wound. Instead, he removes his clown mask and one arm off his sword. Underneath is a dark face, with skin that wraps around the nose, looking phallic in nature. His right eye glows bright yellow, and his left bleeds a dark red.

I hear footsteps from my right, and Sugar Pass slams the sword's handle into my head as I turn my head. I fall onto the dirty ground, still trying to look at who's walking toward me. Before I can, however, a flash of bright yellow flings itself into Sugar Pass. I focus my eyes to see Stephen standing proudly over me. He reaches an arm down, which I grab. He hoists me onto my feet as we both stand looking at Sugar Pass.

"You came. Quite fast, actually," I say.

"Funny thing, after the call, I left the basement, and a blue gateway awaited me and brought me here. I don't even know where it came from!" he jokes back. Sugar Pass wipes some blood off his spiral face, taking off his black suit jacket. Underneath the sleeves are titanium plates, which radiate a transparent blue shield. He slams his arms together, combining the shield pieces into one, as he runs toward Stephen. Sugar Pass rams into Stephen, knocking him down, but I jump onto Sugar Pass' unprotected back.

I grab onto his ears, pulling them back. Sugar Pass lets out a yelp, trying to catch me with his stuck-together arms. I start bashing my furry head into the back of his, denting his skull and hearing the fragments cracking off. I slam my head a few times until I go straight through the skull, feeling my forehead against his slushy brain. I look at his head, seeing a large crater covered in blood and loose hair.

I drop myself from the back of Sugar Pass, letting him fall to his side. Then, I step over his body to help Stephen up, who had just fallen.

"Easy fight, like always," I say. Stephen rolls his eyes, and as we walk toward the exit doors, I hear some rustling behind me. I turn around to see Sugar Pass' head detaching from the neck, with the skin stretching like a thick slime. It wriggles around, and little bony legs sprout from its spine bones. It pushes itself upright, setting its sights on Stephen. I run to cover him, but the little head jumps between my legs, biting his Achilles tendon of

Stephen. The entire mound of the flesh is bitten clean off, and Stephen falls to the ground.

I try to stomp on the head, but it quickly jumps around the room. I chase it in a full circle, and the head jumps onto Stephen's.

"Stop. He's in enough pain. Just let him go, and you can have me," I try to plead, but the head winks at me with one intact eye. "NO!"

Sugar Pass' head drills its bony legs into Stephen's eyes, plucking them out. He throws them across the room, and they roll into the walls. I dive onto the ground, stretching my arms out and grabbing onto Sugar Pass' head. I start to squeeze it, and eventually, my hands come together, popping the fiend. I wipe my hands together, getting the gore off my fingers.

"FUCK," I yell out in anger. I slam my fists into the ground as I stand up. I look down at my bloody body and then at Sugar Pass' dead corpse. I bend over, put my hands on my knees and catch my breath.

"I can't do this anymore. He can have me...and nobody else can get hurt."

I recuperate and walk over to pull the suit off. It's a little complicated, with the titanium arms pushing against the vest. I put the pants on, one leg after the other. I pull them up and tighten them from the inside. Next, I put on the vest and then the suit jacket. It all oddly fits me. I look at the red and blue painted arena around me as I walk through the blood-stained sand out of the large, factory-like doors. I look down both sides of the blinding white steel hallway to see where I came from and check out the other way. I begin walking in the new direction, wiping some sand off my pants. In front of me is a small, gray door with a little blue window. Something calls for my name as I place my hand on its handle.

"Rowan…?" I hear. I look down to my right to see an open vent cover. Two glowing blue eyes stare at me from the darkness. I watch as the feathery arms of Blue Jay reach out to me.

"Maya?" I ask, crouching down and grabbing onto her arm. I pull her out, and she looks horrible. Her blue jumpsuit is covered in grease, blood, and dirt. Her hair is messy and looks sticky. I help her up, and she limps over to hug me. Her arms wrap around my body, and I pat her on the back.

"I'm so glad you're safe," she says. "My powers… they're all taken from me…."

"Ok, ok, just come with me," I say, lifting one of her arms over my shoulder. I walk with her, opening the gray door and entering the next room.

~The Field~

The Star stands in front of his enemy, held against a wall wrapped in chains. The space is damp and cold, with the orange-brown walls seemingly sweating with oozing liquids running down the edges. For someone who has waited for this moment for a long time, he seems disinterested in the encounter.

"What made you lose everything?" he asks an unconscious TV. "I feel that killing you would prove nothing…you are already dead in a sense."

"Sir, we have breaches in the lower areas," a voice says from behind The Star. He turns around to see The Dog, standing in his cardigan with an added holster around the belt.

"I will deal with them later; I have something to attend to now," The Star demands. "I feel lost."

"Why?" The Dog asks, and Star Man scolds him.

"Don't you see? The TV died a long time ago. This man is his body…but a different person overall."

The Star approaches The TV, looking closer into his eyes. He opens them with his fingers and sees cloudy purple eyes, and a black pupil breaks through the smoke and snaps to The Star's position.

"You're still in there," The Star says. The Dog's ears begin to wiggle around.

"Then let's kill him!"

The Dog pulls out a small silver energy pistol from the holster as The Star grabs onto the extended barrel.

"No. Just wait...I have an idea," The Star says to The Dog. He places both hands on The TV's head, his fingers rising in heat. The unconscious TV awakens from the boiling pain, his arms pulsing with green and purple as the chains around him burst into ash. The TV grabs onto The Star's head and throws it onto the ground.

"I still have control of my men. I will bring you back to Roan, and the Commission of Gellax will look at your breaking of the God Code," The TV yells out. His arms beat with his signature double colors until a gust of wind bursts open the door and knocks off his purple fedora. It floats to the ground, and the colors disappear. Before Matthew can react, The Dog pulls the trigger.

A light blue ball of energy erupts from the barrel, pushing into Matthew and detonating inside the small room. The far wall shatters with the explosion, and Matthew's body is flung into the air. Star Man's body is pushed down to the ground, where he manages to escape. The Dog's body hurls the opposite of Matthew's. His body crashes through the door and stumbles down an endless set of stairs onto the top of a fence. The little spikes at the top rip through his stomach, and he lies draped across the wall like a deer.

~~

We enter into a clearing, some sort of zoo enclosure from the looks of it. High, tactile beige walls surround diamond-shaped land. Short, white boxes sit in three corners and the middle. Behind the walls, tall observation towers lack anyone to observe them. The blue sky is a calming departure from the storming city of Usnax. I stand in the middle of the clearing, sensing something. I hear chatter from all around but no life to speak. Maya stands next to me, looking at my face; I can see her in the corner of my eyes. I focus on one of the towers, a tall brown-orange one; I can see stairs leading up to it on the other side. Something's coming from it.

"Rowan?" I hear someone call out. I look to see Harvey running at me. His clothes are torn, and a large cut runs from cheek to cheek. He runs across the sand and grass, dirt spewing from behind his feet.

"Harvey? Where did you-" I'm cut off as the tower I was watching before explodes in a blast of blue light. Large chunks of the wall slam into the ground around us, and I see a body fall. It crashes into the ground, a cloud of sand forming around it. I run over to see the body of Matthew, with dirt and blood smudged across his face. I pick up one of his hands, and for a moment, he appears as…someone. The never-ending droning sound of a heartbeat monitor begins in my head.

"I thought I could save you…I should've let you leave with Stephen…," I say to him. I feel the all too familiar coldness form in his hand.

"We need to go, Rowan; I'm sorry," Harvey says, pulling on my arm. I hesitate to get up but do when the pulling begins to hurt. So we leave Matthew behind, lying frozen on the dirt.

~~

"He is dead," The Star says, looking at The Dog's corpse. The Star shakes his head and pulls the corpse down. The spikes drag through the skin, slicing the rest of the body in half. The Dog falls onto the ground, and The Star watches as Death materializes in front of him.

"Your doing?" Death asks.

"No. His own. Both of them are," The Star says. "I've been so afraid…that I let hate blind me. But The TV was planning to kill me, right?"

The desperation in his voice stands out.

"No, he thought you wanted to kill him," Death responds. The desperation turns to anger.

"He thought that lowly of me?" The Star begins to yell. His yellow four-pointed face shines harsher as his voice loudens. "Then I won. I have to take care of some pests, and then I'll return."

"Magona has risen," Death says, holding an arm over The Dog. The body fades as some black dahlias grow in its place. "You and The Seventh are all left…and he's still remaining in stasis."

"What?" The Star cries out. "How could this happen? The Seventh banished Magona…so long ago."

"A group you indirectly created is trying to stop him," Death says. "But we both know how this will end. The Seventh was right, and we are the reason Magona is here. I'm sorry, but I know soon I'll have to take your body too."

The Star stares into the blue sky, clouds forming over, as Death walks out of view. The Star watches as a black box streaks through, flying across the base. He walks along the edge of the ruined baseball stadium, through the ruined buildings of North Orephia. Contrary to Usnax, Orephia is a city of three-story houses with a closer community. At least, it used to be until The Star set up his operations there. He slowly replaced every person with one he created, and eventually, he felt a small amount of loneliness.

The neighborhoods circle around the Church of Saint Fiacre, a more compact building with a high bell tower over the front entrance. The bell never rings anymore, which adds to the city's silence. He walks through the middle aisle, past the empty pews. Imprints of people remain against the wood.

The Star steps onto the raised platform where the main altar sits. He stands behind it, looking at the dim room. He's reminded of how he used to stand here, protecting people against the patriarchal system he tried to adapt to. The Star attempted to be a public figure, a mayor almost. He wanted to prove that his death would be fatal, but after his plans failed, he just waited until The TV came for him.

Nobody was prepared for the accusations about psychiatric hospitals across the world. People accused and

166

complained about the poor treatment, the misogynistic staff, and total government funding. The Star wanted to cut it only after the statements came out, but The Dog said the people could easily be replaced. Slowly, one by one, The Star did so. City after city, all populated with exact copies, but with the mindset of The Star. He couldn't do anything about the government since he replaced the first, and The Dog was in charge of it all.

Eventually, when the hospitals and jails filled up, The Star took it upon himself to undo the effects he had caused. He tried to round up all the monsters he created from the gym incident and, with the help of a scientist, tried to remove their powers. The tests backfired, and they put too much into their systems. The Star accidentally created worse but was able to control them. He used them as generals, more potent than the simple military twins but not as strong as The Star.

They would go around the world to capture whoever they could find, but eventually, it became a challenge. The leader of the Dextrose Division, Sugar Pass, was able to completely wipe the United States as well as Germany within one month. The leader of the Lurking Shadow division, Phantom Guerilla, stormed Usnax and took over the Northern and Southern areas before returning to home base due to unknown reasons.

All during this, The Star would sit and wait. He would wait for The TV to find him, but it eventually took too long. The Star began to think that The TV gave up and thought about returning to Roan a lot. But something kept The Star on Earth. Whispers in his area and a ghostly presence around him would manipulate him into staying. It would feed The Star words of encouragement to get The TV to his location and to keep The Dog close by.

Then, when he found The TV's body washed up on his base, he knew that the voice somehow brought them together. Another general, Box Master, located a few others scattered around and imprisoned them in the sewers while sending them through their past for information. One of them was a character named Biiko, a Flauer creature from the planet Ostarus. They are a race of wooden skeletal frames with a face of pedals and teeth. Biiko, in particular, is a ribcage with a singular arm hanging on the side. The spine wiggles down into a bony foot that it hops around on. A green stem wraps around some of the bones and supports a spiky yellow pedal face, with a mouth in the middle. They use the pedals to sense movements and waves in the air to see.

Biiko was captured and tortured like the rest, but not from a portal. Instead, Biiko found themself in a situation when traversing a greenhouse. They were spotted by a brute, one of Sugar Pass's. While Box Master was sending them through their past, a brute alerted him of Rowan. He left the room, leaving Biiko alone, where they were able to squeeze out of the chains. They ran through the sewer, hopping on their foot until they found a staircase opposite the one leading to Sugar Pass's arena.

Box Master returned to the cell to see Biiko gone and rushed back to Rowan's to see him nowhere. He tried to alert The Star, who was busy talking to Death. Box Master ran to tell Sugar Pass, who he found dead on the ground. So he decided to lock the building down, running to the main server room where a woman in a blue jumpsuit floats in a large, water-filled tank.

As The Star stands at the altar, he hears sirens blasting outside. Running out into the streets, he sees a metal dome on top of the stadium. Red lights flash around the walls, and the doors are all secured with steel planks. He can swiftly squeeze through one of the shutting doors as the entire building is closed off to the outside. The white lights inside all shut-off, switching back on with a dark red.

The Star runs through the empty stadium tunnels, past the gated-off stores and blocked-off corridors to the inside field. He finds the central control room, a large chamber with servers and control modules lining the walls. Empty desk chairs dot the floor, and Box Master stands over a large lever, which sparks as he holds the broken top half.

"What have you done?" The Star yells at him. Box Master jumps and turns around, dropping the lever piece.

"I-I'm sorry, I tried contacting you," he stutters. The Star pushes him aside and tries to push the lever, but it's lodged in place. He angrily turns to Box Master, who tries to run out of the room. The Star grabs onto the back of his shirt, pulling him back. Box Master slams into some servers, loose wires being flung out. The Star pulls him up by his collar and grabs one of the sparking wires. Finally, he shoves it into Box Master's mouth, and his neck begins to shine red.

Box Master chokes on the electricity, and his eyes become bloodshot. Blood pools out of his mouth as he shakes around, the electricity running through his body. The Star absorbs it all, sending it back through the exposed wires. Box Master's eyes finally pop, blood squirting onto The Star's shiny face. He lets go of Box Master's collar; his body slams onto the ground with a thud. The Star angrily punches the indented server as he storms out of the room, going straight for the main elevator.

~~

We take shelter in a small dim closet, next to shelves of cleaning supplies and a stiff mop. I hold Matthew's purple fedora, which seems to shine despite the low lighting. I flip it over, and on the inside is something I've never noticed. A small needle in the very middle. It's exceptionally missable, but it shines a deep purple color. I press my finger onto it, and it pricks me. I quickly put my finger in my mouth to lick any blood that I may be leaking. I look at the cut, which I notice isn't there. Instead, a small purple circle lies at the edge of my pointer finger. In fact, I see the purple ring on the fur of each finger. Maya and Harvey don't seem to notice; in fact, Maya seems to be different. She hasn't spoken since I found her and hasn't really done anything yet.

~~

Biiko finds themself in some sort of server room, with an eyeless corpse on the ground. They walk around the destruction, finding a tank with a floating woman inside. Biiko smashes its shaky hand into the glass, which forms a small crack. A little spout of water begins to shoot out, drenching Biiko and being absorbed through their roots.

The woman sinks down to the bottom of the tube, slowly waking up and scratching her head. She sees a flower creature and doesn't overthink it.

"Excuse me, what is your name?" Biiko asks in a scratchy, warped voice.

"You can talk?" the woman asks in surprise. "My name is Maya...and I need to return to Usnax."

"Don't bother; there's nothing left for you there. And besides, we cannot get out; the place is in lockdown," Biiko cries out. "All we can do now is wait to die."

~~

There's a knock on the closet door. It's light at first, and then it gets more aggressive. None of us act to open it, hoping they'll walk by.

"Hello?" a voice calls out. I recognize it, but my mind blanks on who it belongs to. "I watched you three run in... who's the girl?"

"Maya?" Harvey asks. "It can't be; she's right here."

We both look over at Maya, who's dripping with sweat. Strands run down her face and neck, and her hair is soaked. The figure knocks again and tries to twist the doorknob open. We had secured the door by putting the back of a chair under it. The doorknob twists and turns as the door is violently pushed against. Maya slowly bends her head forward and kicks the leg of the chair. Then, it flings into a shelf of labeled bottles. Then, in a matter of seconds, a lot happens.

Firstly, a woman bursts through the door that looks precisely like Maya. Second, the Maya with us grabs onto Harvey and quickly drags him out of the room. Lastly, the shelf falls onto me, and the glass bottles all shatter against the ground. Liquids and small rocks splash against my skin, my fur burning away until even my skin is affected. The outside Maya runs over to me and pulls me out from the fallen rack.

I slide over the spilled canisters, my purple suit torn open from the acidic liquids I find myself in. She drags me to the far wall, next to a boarded door to the stadium field.

"Maya?" I ask. "But you were just with us."

"That wasn't me, Rowan," she says. I look past her to see the dirty Maya that was with us standing in a pool of red blood. I push Maya out of the way to see the other one holding onto something in her hand. She holds onto the severed head of Harvey, holding it from the spine, the head dangling down with a frozen look of terror. The blood drips onto the ground.

"I made her while I studied the real one," someone says from behind me. I see The Star walking toward us around a bend, clapping his yellow hands. His blank, four-pointed face shines upon us; a ring around his head looks like a halo. "You all must realize something...these powers are a curse. You should know that, right?"

"I know what you tried to do to me," my Maya yells through clenched teeth. She runs from me toward The Star, a fist readied and a lust for blood. Wings appear on her back, and she flies into the air. "You tried to put me in a torture asylum...the same cell my mother was in. I watched you pay off the judge both times I had to go to court. I felt trapped...and only when I used my abilities did I feel free."

"I remember you too. You see, I only kept the direct line of finance because even with the abuse and arisen problems...it was the only place I could keep your kind," The Star explains as his blue suit melts into his yellow body. "I couldn't let them run rampant...I mean...I should know what it's like for someone to be lost for too long."

"Your feelings of being astray will not last for much longer," Maya says as she slowly flaps her wings, moving closer to The Star. Instead, he puts a single finger up, inches away from Maya's face.

"You won't want to kill me."

"Why's that?" Maya asks. The Star lowers his arm, and the yellow skin begins to throb. Yellow fingers pop out of his elbow, and pale skin slowly wraps around them, the fingers pushing outward, with an arm following. A leg falls to the ground, and a body erupts from the yellow skin. An elderly woman is molded out of The Star's arm. A long, blue gown slowly appears over her body, and long black hair grows from her head.

She walks toward Maya with open arms.

"My little Maya-pie," she says. Maya steadily floats to the ground, where she stares at the woman.

"I can bring anyone back," The Star says, subtly looking over at me. "Even if I've never seen them."

I blink, and I find myself back in my bedroom. A small room with a singular bed in the middle on the wall. A door on my left and one to the bathroom behind me. The purple light from outside and blue wallpaper give the room a very underwater look. I see my wife in the corner, but her appearance is blurry to me. Someone stands in front of me, a child. Black hair, emerald green eyes, rosy cheeks, and a heartwarming smile. He wears a purple suit similar to mine.

"Look! I look like you, dad!" he says. A smile trembles onto my face. I kneel down, and I put my hand on his head.

"You look so good. Go kill it tonight, ok?" I say to him. He smiles and runs out of the room. I look over to my spouse, who I still can't make out. All I can see of her is a smile. It's the same kind of half-smile as when I held her hand last...

"He has your sense of style, sadly," she jokingly says. It gets a chuckle out of me. I try to walk over to her, but my feet don't move. They seem to stick to the ground. "Can you believe he'll be ten tomorrow?"

"Why can't I move?" I cut in. Her smile grows.

"I bet you're glad he was born in a triple-zero year... it's easier to remember his age!" she says. Part of her face becomes more apparent, and I see the familiar brown eyes and dark brown hair.

"Why can't I MOVE," I say again. I look at my legs again, and the floor beneath me sinks down. I quickly turn my head up, seeing her face has completely disappeared, and so have the bed and doors. The blank purple walls around me lose their color, becoming a dark gray.

"PLEASE!" I call out as I continue to sink. The floor makes it up to my waist as I try to push myself out. "I just want them BACK; get me OUT!"

Her smile appears above me as I feel my chin touch the carpet.

"He loves you," is the last thing I hear as I'm blinded by darkness. In my head, I hear my son's voice one more time, but I can't seem to understand what he says. I hope it's worth it.

~The Supernova~

Just another sun cycle on Roan, as normal as it gets.

Green skies and purple light. Although, today was especially cold. The breeze didn't help either, my yellow legs having goosebumps along them.

"Hard day for you, huh?" The TV asks me. He leans on the balcony we both stand on, overlooking the Main City of Roan. It's a bustling day, probably due to the routes for trade being open again after maintenance. Ships of all kinds fly down through the green clouds to stop at the edge's landing pads. The TV and I stand on the balcony of The Angelic.

Today, like most days, The Angelic is out with his followers. They developed a religion, passed on from Earth II, and he twists it in his own way. He paints himself as a savior, which I think is a little odd. But, it doesn't harm anyone. They usually practice their beliefs in an underground temple around Roan's core.

"What about you? All those tests on humans…and what? You can't even interact with them," I say back to him. "I'd say The Seventh has a better job than you."

"Yeah? Well, hey, I'm just saying that if humans were ever in some catastrophe, they'd be able to survive," The TV tries to explain. "Just give them a few thousand years."

It would be just like this every day. I would watch the cities as the other Gods would do their duties until our trust was challenged one day. This day began more normal than the others. Green sky, calming breeze, booming economy. But as I stand on the balcony admiring the system we have built, Death approaches me.

"The Star, we need your say in a serious matter," he says, his voice very stern.

"What's the matter?" I ask, joining him in taking an elevator down to the surface, where the Commission of Gellax is. We walk the maze-like hallways of the ruined, beige undercrofts until we reach the immense double black gate doors. I push through them, seeing The Seventh kneeling on the floor, his wrists wrapped in mysterious bindings. His head hangs low as three of the committee chairs are filled. The TV, The Crusher, and The Dog sit watching The Seventh. Death and I sit in another two chairs, leaving two more open.

"Where is The Angelic?" I ask The TV, who silences me with a shush. I look around the chamber, the white and gold painted arches and pillars around the circular room. The chairs are all raised up, towering over whoever is being tried. Today, The Seventh is being tested.

"The Seventh. The Seventh God who brought nothing to the table is now being accused of banishing The Angelic to the Plane of Celestial," The TV calls out, standing at his seat.

"P-please, he exiled my wi-," The Seventh tries to plead.

"SILENCE!" The TV screams out, which shuts The Seventh's mouth. "Your wife went missing several days ago, and you use it as your excuse now? We found you with the Tophet Sword, and in the last place The Angelic was seen."

"It's his fault; I-I didn't do anything," The Seventh tries again to say.

"We only keep you on this team because Gellax made you for something, but it seems like he had a lapse in judgment, hm?" The TV snarks. The Crusher and The Dog both snicker. "Since we cannot send you to the Plane of Celestial as that would be a breach of our God Code…you will be forever trapped in stasis as a reminder."

"To who? Who will be reminded that the Tophet Sword gets you trapped FOREVER?" The Seventh yells out. "None of you will wield it…only The Angelic will. Or should I call him Magona?"

"Do NOT speak of Magona," The TV yells out. "Magona is a false belief system; you know it too."

"When will we get to the freezing process?" The Crusher butts in. "I want him in my place."

"You'll regret this," The Seventh says as he stands up and a glass frame appears around him. They connect until a rectangular glass chamber locks him in place. He closes his eyes as he is frozen inside, and The TV walks down with his jar and staff. He puts it in an open spot next to The Seventh, and the items are also trapped.

I watch as The Crusher picks up the entire glass container with The Seventh inside, bringing it into the undercrofts and presumably to his asylum. The rest of the Gods leave as well, except for The TV.

"Did we make a good decision?" I ask him.

"Of course we did; he acted without reason," The TV says as he stretches on his golden throne. I nod and walk down the corridors, where I turn a corner and discover myself at my church altar. The pews are filled with citizens; some even have to stand in the back.

"What will you do about the hospital?" one woman calls out.

"Should we pray today?" another cries.

"Please calm down," I try to say, but the people chant louder, and the lights flicker. Everyone's voices sound more demonic as they yell, and their faces melt into horrifying blank ashy faces. They start to climb over the pews toward me, to which I hide under the altar. They eventually reach me and begin to pull me out by my legs. I try to break free when my body lights up until the room is blinding and a shockwave is sent through the church. Everyone is blasted back, and their bodies pop, blood and gore streaking across the walls. Then, I climb onto the altar, looking around at the mess of corpses strewn about the place.

"It's ok, I can fix this," I say to myself as I begin to birth copies of every one. Then, before I can get a single arm out of mine, Death places a bony hand on my blue-suited shoulder.

"You can't keep replacing everyone. You need to learn that you're abusing this power…," he says to me. "I understand your motives…but you need to come clean instead of sweeping everything under the rug."

"I can't keep doing this… I'm in over my head, and you know that" I plead to him. "I want to go back, but he'll just follow me and kill me."

"You need to take responsibility for everything you've done and the people you have hurt," Death responds. "You may not like it, but without them, you'd be floating around space with nothing to do."

"Death, what really happened with Magona?" I ask him. The answer has always haunted me. "Did we make a good decision banishing The Seventh?"

"We have been crumbling from the inside out ever since Gellax made us."

And with that, Death does his job, and I walk out of the church. As the doors open, the area outside spins until it becomes the standard room of a court. Brown walls, a judge stand, and yellow circular lights shining down on a crowd of angry civilians. They all scream at me and throw wrappers, empty cups, and other miscellaneous objects toward my place as the speaker. I tap on the bendy microphone in front of me as I bend over to speak clearly into it.

"I would like to state that…after some thorough inspection of the Eastern Usnax Psychiatric Hospital, no exploits were found. In our studi-," I start. I'm cut off as the room erupts with curses and yells. I look around the red-faced crowd, my eyes set on one singular woman sitting down. Her teary eyes stare into mine as I try to calm the crowd. The image of her face blinks in and out with the same woman but in the present.

"You expect me to like this…," she says. She looks at me and then back at the twin of her mother. "When you're the reason she died?"

"There was never any concrete evidence," I try to say. Maya slaps her mother out of the way, to which she falls onto the ground, and her head cracks open. "Listen, I was on your side."

"Really?" Maya screams out. "I watched you that day when you justified the mistreatment she went through."

Her face flickers back to the courtroom for only a moment, and the crowd has disappeared, and only her face remains.

"But she is back now, and Rowan, I can bring back anyone YOU want!" I try to plead with them more. Rowan turns his head away, tending to his burns.

"My son lies with my heart…and if the universe wanted it that way, so be it," Rowan says from under his breath. I try to reach out to Maya.

"Don't touch me," she says, backing away. "I don't know if I should kill you now or leave you to die."

As the impact of her words hit me, so does a large gust of wind. It blows through the halls, but Maya's stare at me doesn't break. Another blast comes from the left, and I cease my concentration to look at Rowan. He's slumped over like before, but I notice Death standing over him. His yellow bones...tattered brown cloak...blue stitches down his ribs and skull.

"Him?" I ask.

"You care for him?" Death asks me.

"I...," I start. "I don't want to be evil anymore. I'm just scared...I have been since we trapped The Seventh. I've been afraid that I could go down that path...and I probably almost did."

"It doesn't excuse what you did," Maya yells. Death crouches down next to Rowan.

"It won't...but it's not for us to judge," Death says. He holds up Rowan's head, and we look at his frozen smile. Closed eyes...raised lips...missing patches of hair everywhere...but still wearing the purple fedora. "He's always had his family around. Even if he didn't know it."

"What now, Death?" I ask. "None of us can win now. The battle that never was has ended."

"I think we both know what has to happen," Death says as Rowan fades away. A patch of purple gardenias grows through cracks under where he was. "You are all that's left. The Angelic is technically dead…Magona is all that remains."

"Could we stop him, Death?" I ask, pulling myself up to my feet. "You're still here; maybe we coul-"

"No," Death states. "I only exist as a spirit now. If The Seventh was still with us, he could. Enjoy the time you have left. Fix your mistakes. Ok?"

Death fades as well, and I am left with Maya. She looks at me, and her expression has changed. She's still angry but has a small amount of understanding to it. We both walk out into the ruins of a once-great city. The blue sky shines down on the gray buildings, and the blinding sun lights everything up. I run my hand along dusty walls as we walk with no destination.

We reach the border, and more specifically, the ocean. Maya takes one last look at me with a look of goodbye and repentance. Wings grow out from her back, and she flaps into the air. She flies into the sky, traveling over the ocean and into the horizon. But, on the other hand, I stay back at the stadium as I hear cracking from the server room.

I step in, seeing rats nibbling at Box Master's remains. I also see new cracks in the walls that leak out blue light. Streaks of the blue shoot into the middle of the room, where a purple rectangle is formed. It lets out a robotic droning noise, and the light spills onto the ground. The gateway seems unstable, with the shape having fractured pieces all around the edges.

I step through, winding up in a dense forest. The wind softly blows across my shining face as the sound of chirping birds fills my ears. A view of snow-topped mountains can be observed past the towering sequoia trees. I step over a patch of purple lilac flowers, seeing a few figures in the distance. I keep my space, hiding behind a brown tree trunk, watching a yellow-skinned man lay his bony red-skinned man against a trunk.

"That's them," Death says from behind me. I don't turn to look at him. "Some of your actions brought them together, and they got through one of Magona's defenses."

"Redd?" I hear the yellow man call out, and they both embrace each other.

"So we still failed?" I ask.

"We failed a long time ago," Death confirms.

The red man slides onto the grass as Death walks over.

"I am sorry, L," he says. His voice sounds sincere, like always. "You saved us."

The yellow man doesn't respond and waits in the grass for Death to let the red man fade. Pink chrysanthemums dot the tree as Death lifts his hood and walks back to me.

"It's only the beginning, Star. We can be brought back somehow," Death guesses.

The yellow man looks up at the yellow sun, which shines upon his equally colored face. I also look up at the sky, seeing it swiftly turn orange, as if the sunset within seconds. He slowly lays on the ground, closing his eyes as Death approaches him. The yellow man's space is overgrown with yellow solidasters, and Death's job finishes as he fades. The wind picks up, and the leaves begin to violently thrash around.

Cracks form under my feet, orange light shining up from them. I look up to see two ghostly white figures standing between the trees. One looks like The Dog, and the other...The TV.

"How...are you two here?" I ask.

"Our souls are now trapped here. Magona has started the Reaping of Form, and all souls, physical or not, are now trapped to stay here as it burns," The TV says, his voice sounding echoey. "And, you are too."

I don't respond.

Instead, I look at the sky, seeing a flash of black and orange shoot into the sky, where it disappears in a gleam of blue. The ground under me trembles as I feel my soul rip from my body, and I join the rest.

Trapped in the Soul Prison of Earth II.

~~

Magona steps from a blue gateway onto the coarse Earth dirt. His gaping mouth and heavy breathing silence all other loose sounds. The distant smoke and blue sky put a smile on his bumpy face. The gateway closes behind him, spinning into nothing. He holds his unfinished orange-bladed sword next to his black robes. He glides the shattered tip against the ground, cracks forming underneath.

"This is…perfect. Three in one place…as long as my gateways have worked as I hoped," he says in a slow and monotone voice. The dense hills and ruined trees around him shake as he holds the hilt with both hands. He raises the sword above his head and brings it down to the crust. The ground erupts into orange electricity as the dirt cracks and explodes into the dense air. Magona floats up as he watches Earth crumble from the blow.

Another blue gateway opens behind him as he hovers into space, watching the blue and green shatter into molten rocks. He passes by the dark void of space, phasing through the gateway. He appears in a temple on Roan, where his army of devoted followers bow before him, all donned in dark robes and cloaks. They all pray to him as they ready themselves for the journey ahead. Before the departure, however, Magona makes sure to take one last look at the body in stasis in the asylum.

"Everything you had, I took," he says to himself, smiling. As one final gateway opens on the purple dunes of Roan and Magona's cult travel through, the blue spark in the jar dims and shrinks, and the green husk's insides beat faster.

~The Epilogue~

"The Gods have fallen."

The screams of a trillion souls reached every corner of the universe. People of all sorts of races and types mourned all at once. The departed, however, were finally laid to rest as their bodies evaporated in the almost complete freedom of Roan. However, the sacrifices of L, Red, and their group were unknown by the public, and their names were never repeated.

People feel unprotected.

With bad news comes worse; a dictator named Lord Daytör collected the wreckage with his family of one mother and two brothers. While scrounging through, he found shards of an ancient artifact that he had been looking for for a very long time. At the same point as that, however, someone was being interviewed.

A tall, dark-haired man sits on a cold, metal chair. His short hair and bald spot make his head look like a mangled bird's nest. A sparkling black suit rests upon his body. He sits in a dark room, with only a dim overhead light to see. In front of him is a desk, a short one, with a file lying atop it. Across from him sits a woman with scarred, pulsing skin across the right of her body. The long, void-black hair covers her face, but her frowning mouth and half-red lips peek out. Her outfit consists of a black corset, black leggings, and black boots.

"Did you hear Roan is free now?" the man asks with a voice of clear crispness. He folds his arms onto his legs and stares at her.

"Still not a tourist destination," the woman says quietly.

"Earth perished, as well," the man follows up. The woman looks at him and tilts her head.

"You actually care about that place? Even more worthless than Roan."

"Who are you?" the man quickly asks.

"Shouldn't you know?" the woman asks. Her voice sounds demanding and cold like she did something wrong. She lifts her head up, letting the hair drip to one side of her face. The scars are hidden while her purple glowing left eye shows. The man sighs, moving his arms to the file.

"Your name is Janx, correct? Janx Jentree? 'A hired assassin,' it says here." So he turns the file around and towards the woman, pointing to a page about her. Paperclipped to the paper is a mugshot of her from when she was a teenager. "What is it that brought you to kill for money?"

"You answered your own question," she says. The man clenches his lips together and nods. "I do it for the money. Being good at this job pays well, and a ship off of here costs a fortune."

"You want to get off this planet?" The man pulls a small notepad out of his suit pocket and bites some skin off of his left pointer finger. He begins to write on the tablet with the blood, smearing it into legible words.

"I want to go to the moons of Tacamow, where I can own some farmland and just grow shit." The woman stares past the man as she thinks about Tacamow, a lush, green planet with acres of farmland and a population of seventy-three. She grows a smile, just as she would a plant.

"Is there something on your tooth?" the man cuts in. A slight bulge wraps itself around the surface of the woman's two front teeth. Her smile fades as she stares into the man's eyes. "Apologies. Continue."

The woman continues to talk about her dreams as the man pulls a small box radio out from his pants pocket. He holds down a button on the side, whispering too quietly for the woman to hear. A few seconds later, an unlit door opens behind the man, letting natural light in. He turns around to see a small, plump creature walk in. It's a round body with stubby feet, fingerless hands, and one large mouth covering the front. It has two small eyes on the top of its head, which blink sporadically.

Behind him, a silhouette stands in the doorway.

"She has the qualifications for the job. Now, I must be going; I have a meeting with some frie-," the man is cut off as the woman pulls the bulge from her teeth, revealing it to be a tangled wire. She straightens it and jumps across the table, wrapping it around his neck. She pulls it back hard, and the man shoots his hands up to his throat, but she is too strong. The wire breaks through the skin, seeping blood from the throat onto the clean black suit.

His head drops down, and the woman lets go, and the body hits the desk first, denting it, then the ground.

"You did that fast. I thought you would've waited until he gave you the thumbs up," the silhouette speaks from the light.

"I'm efficient," the woman says, wiping blood from her hands onto her leggings. "What was his name again?"

"You didn't read the file?"

"I never do. You'll have to get used to that," the woman snaps back.

"His name is-well, WAS Goay-N. I hired him to be my eyes on the streets. To look for any people worthy enough," the silhouette explains. "He was right about you. This was your first job, and you already killed him within five minutes of the meeting."

"Why did you want me to kill your own man?" the woman cuts in. The silhouette laughs, and the small round creature sneezes.

"He's part of a group that gives themselves away TOO easily."

"Are they dangerous?" I ask him.

"Depends on who you ask," he laughs. "And I say…no. So listen to me. I have some jobs for you. And you'll do them, or else."

~~

Silence. The lights make no sound, nor does my breathing. Only the sound of the running water meets my ears. I wash the blood off my arms with the dirty sink water while staring at my face in the cracked mirror. My long black hair is tangled up in a mess, bloody tears stream down my cheeks, and I pick a broken tooth out of my mouth. I brush the dirt off my ripped black corset and matching black leggings. The grime floats to the ground, where I kick it away with my knee-high black boots. I finish washing in the dirty, molding, green bathroom as I walk back into the nightclub. The shitty modern music of Loca fills my ears and drowns out everything else.

Purple and blue spotlights move around the floor as the only lighting inside, illuminating the patrons. Drunk dancers and desperate dick-havers take up every last corner as I push through them. The Lükahmp Nightclub is everyone's favorite place to go to get smashed and to smash. I mean, who doesn't love the cramped interior, the bar with any kind of drink, and the stripper section. I only go for one reason.

My employer works here.

I make my way through the litter-covered floor to the bar and pool table. A group of five Dismayed Waltzers set up a pool game as I take a seat in one of the spinny steel red bar seats. The blue and purple spotlights criss-cross the bar in front of me, but my eyes have already gotten used to the darkness. A yellow Zargon walks up to me, setting down a brown glass bottle of Streamo. I've never been fond of the dragon-like Zargons, with their long necks, big horns, and appetite for human meat, but I can manage when they're in a crowded area. I take a sip of the Streamo and feel the familiar sweet, honey-like taste hit my tongue. I swallow and set the bottle down on the hardwood counter as I see something sit next to me from the corner of my eye.

"You ready?" he asks. 'He' being my employer, Marz. A literal gangster monkey from another planet, his breed is a genetically altered tamarin, and his fur is all brown with a long beard-like white puff on his chin. He wears an eyepatch and has old, forgotten scars etched into his back. He speaks to me without turning his head to look at me.

"Who, where, and when. That's all I need to know," I respond to him as I take another sip of the Streamo. Marz slides a folder over to me, and I open it up. Inside is a paper full of details, and a photo is connected to it via a paperclip. An alarming photo. A pale, moon-like-skinned man with a long brown beard with hair tied up in a man bun. A missing nose, with ripped flesh where it should be, beginning between the eyes and returning to flesh above the top lip. Dark brown sunglasses. A steel jaw, mold colored. The name at the top of the file reads' Seventh Hunter.' The rest of the text under it blurs in my mind. I know information is needed to understand why I should kill someone, but I'd instead not feel anything for the victim.

"A dirty man goes by the name of Julia-N. Used to work at Al-X's casino and lives in an underground bunker near Carishem. He's part of an underground revolution. You should remember I told you about it," Marz says as I examine the photo. I nod my head in confirmation, although it's a lie. I remember the base details he gave me, but not any specifics.

Al-X. The boss of the 'Get Rich Casino.'

"I uploaded the location to your ultario," Marz adds before he swings off the chair. Before waddling off to the dance floor, he throws a few sugola coins onto the counter. I raise my left arm and swipe from elbow to wrist with my right hand, accidentally rubbing a cut I forgot I had. An inch-wide hole opens in my palm, and a hologram lights up from it. A holographic map of Loca dimly lights my face as I zoom in on the new marker. I pass all the significant landmarks displayed in 3D with minor scanlines, right to the Province of Carishem.

A large city, the second-largest on Loca, with the most amount of corruption in the entire Ikenin system. Home to the Get Rich Casino, a seventy-story building built right in the middle of the city. The Province of Carishem has existed for thousands of years and is also home to the most devious Locanagwans of all time. Nobody knows the entire true history of the city, but all I know is the mayor, Valure Eroper, cares only about money. Hell, the city's motto is "Only the RICH make money." This will be the first time I've ever stepped into this asswipe of a town, and I'm not looking forward to it.

—

Seven thousand by ten thousand miles. That is the dimensions of the moss-covered brick wall surrounding the lush Province of Carishem. One singular entrance is the only way to get in without breaking Valure's laws. Speaking of the entrance, I was at it now. The large, thousand-foot high wall had a small, six-foot-tall door guarded by a Draphanoid.

Draphanoids are short, plump creatures with robotic skeletons. They're usually around three feet tall and quite fat for such a small creature. Their eyes are atop their heads, and their arms extend from the front of the torso instead of the usual side like most Locanagwan folk.

This Draphanoid is purple, has a red mohawk, and has on some sort of black leather jacket, complete with chains wrapped around its waist like a belt. It stands guard in front of the door, holding a small stick. I can tell it's staring me down, with its eyes slightly covered by the fleshy eyelids. I walk across the grassy walkway, passing by the endless sea of green around me up to the demanding wall of stone. Sounds of soft crunching and the soft kiss of the wind are all I can hear. I make my way up to the Draphanoid, which doesn't flinch or move.

"I would like entry, please," I firmly say. I wait for a response, but the Draphanoid continues to stay still. I walk around it without taking my eyes off. The door is just

194

in reach as the Draphanoid seemingly snaps into reality and throws the stick at me. It pierces my right kneecap, which I scream and fall onto the grass in response; I latch my hands onto the wound as I try to stop the blood flow.

"State your business," the Draphanoid says, its low, demonic-sounding voice cutting the wind like a knife. I look at it, strands of hair dangling in front of my eyes.

"I request…Entry," I respond through clenched teeth. The Draphanoid stares past my eyes as it walks past me to the door. I hear it open behind me, but I don't move until the Draphanoid walks back into view.

"You wait for my response. I was about to speak, but you showed your impatience. You have paid for your crime. Have a good time."

I grab the stick with a firm grip and rip it out of my kneecap. Another scream is let out, and so is another squirt of blood. Nonetheless, I rise to my feet and brush my hair behind my ears. I spin around and limp through the door, which slams behind me. And just like that, I find myself in the Province of Carishem.

—

As I have said before, I have never stepped into the Province of Carishem. It has remained a corrupt and shitty city since before I was born. I have never learned why it became the way it is, but I have overheard certain parts.

The city is separated into three major sections, each part inside the other. On the outer square are the richest lifeforms and the ones with a slow income source. In the middle of the square are the ones with a fair amount of money and a fair income source. The absolute center of Carishem is the poorest of the city, but the ones with a significant and fast income source and the most political power.

They are so poor because of the shining beacon, Al-X's casino. Everyone in the center has such fast income streams that they spend it all in seconds gambling, hence where their overall poor wallets come from. Since the city is so large, the farther from the casino you get, the more prosperous the people are. Since the casino is so far from the city's outskirts, most people living on the outer edges stay in their houses and only spend their money in food markets. Some on the outer sections of town do gamble, but they're few and far between.

Each section has its own distinct look. The border rim is mostly stone huts, makeshift houses made of tree bark, or underground bunkers. The middle area is a bit more classy, with more shiny white quartz decorating the banks, marketplaces, and stores. The center is made of the rarest minerals of Loca, such as hedenuraty, a complex, transparent green rock found in the lower parts of any Locanagwan mines. Mixed with quartz, the houses and shops surrounding the casino shine white and green no matter the number of moons in the sky.

Now, onto the casino.

Al-X is a wealthy man who works the casino by himself. The building is exceptionally tall, and each floor has the cleanest glass in the galaxy. Each floor has hundreds of machines, some big enough for creatures to be inside, such as the large bowling arena on the seventeenth floor, which uses tied-up Zargons as bowling pins. The outside of the casino is decorated with giant neon signs that show advertisements from all across Loca and its bordering moons. As of now, only one promotion has caught my eye.

On the front side of the building, a large screen displays the mayor's face with the words GAMBLE AND WIN BIG. With a fat face that looks almost like a mask, with skin stretched over sunken eyes with an empty glare, Valure Eroper has changed over the years. When I was a child, I would see his broadcasts on the holographs in school, and he used to be skinny. Then, around my teenage years, he stopped making broadcasts, and when he returned a decade ago, he came back bloated and overweight.

—

As I march through the first section, the depressing sight of sleepless nobody's wallowing through their chores. Scratching mold out of the cracks of stone walls. Watering the spiky flowers that bloom from the uneven pathways through houses. Carrying baskets of unknown fruit atop their heads, the destination is also unknown. Nobody seems to blink, nor does anyone seem to be alive. To me, I see animated corpses fitting in with the shadows of the ones that used to strive here. Before the corruption, of course.

I swipe my arm again to check my map, to see how close I am. A small popup of text reads MARKER IN 500 FEET – LEFT. I keep the map open as I walk through crowds of faceless creatures and overgrown stone huts as I find a hatch in the ground near the far bottom left corner of the city wall. A small, iron, rust-colored trapdoor with a dirty circular window in the center and a handlebar on the side. I check my map once more, the marker begins blinking, and another text popup appears. DESTINATION REACHED.

I close the map by swiping my arm the opposite way, pulling the bar up. It's cumbersome, so I pull it with both hands. I let go as it crashes onto the ground opposite me and cracks the stones it lands on. The hole underneath the hatch is just darkness, with a ladder that peaks its sides from the void. I look around to ensure nobody is following me, not that I think I was even noticed, especially this far from the populated areas.

I take a deep breath and grab onto my left finger, cracking it backward until it touches the back of my hand. The nail begins to glow, illuminating a few inches down the hole. Then, as I hold my left hand up and retreat into the depths, sparkles of light shine off the almost entirely rusted ladder.

—

The temperature is hot down here compared to the soft breeze on the surface. Are there any vents here?

A half-eaten purple Zargon corpse decorates a table in the small, underground, concrete bunker. The only noise is the sound of buzzing flies crowding around the yellow lights in the ceiling. The bunker is small, with three main, bare rooms with dirty, light gray walls. No windows, no furniture other than the middle room table and the singular left room bed. The door to the right room is closed, and I shuffle toward it. I keep my watch as I crawl along the walls, making sure nobody could see me if they walk in. Once I reach the door, I slowly reach my hand onto the doorknob. Sweat drips from my forehead as the temperature in the bunker builds up. Without thinking about it, I turn the knob and burst through the door to see an empty room. Nothing, not even light, shows itself.

I hold my glowing nail in front of me to illuminate the room, but it remains dark. I back out of the mysterious room into something which reacts to my touch. I swiftly turn around to see nothing but a shadow creeping at me from the opposite doorway. I stay frozen for a moment, trying to figure out what I'm looking at.

I move my head an inch forward, and the shadow slides out of view. I feel my eyebrows crunch down over my eyes as I bolt out of my statued state, and I dive over the middle table, knocking over the maggot-infested Zargon corpse. I hit the ground with my arms in front of me as I slide into the room with the bed. Once I come to a stop, I roll over onto my chest to face the dirty concrete ceiling. The room contains the previously stated bed, with stained sheets halfway on the ground, a cracked sink dripping with brown water behind the doorway, and a green folded-up metal chair that rests against the wall behind the bed.

Strangely, the shadowy figure is not in the room. I think I am just seeing things until I hear a noise. A whisper. My skin goes pale, and my pupils shrink as I turn my head to the toilet bed. A face looks at me from behind the sheets, shrouded by darkness. I feel my head grow dizzy as a hand reaches itself towards me from under the bed. The hand continues, with an arm following but never stopping. The arm keeps extending and extending, and I begin to scramble upward. Then, I grab onto the doorframe, launching myself towards the ladder as the hand grabs onto my right leg.

It pulls my leg backward, causing me to fall flat onto the pavement floor. I pull my head back up and cover my nose, which is now pointing left and heavily bleeding. The blood fills my mouth as I blink some red out of my eyes. I squish my nose in between my palms and crack my nose back into place, which causes me to scream in pain. I quickly slap myself as I kick the hand with my left foot.

It lets go, and I launch myself onto the ladder, slamming into the metal pegs. One slams into my left eye, but I just suck up the pain and climb up. My finger light continues to shine the way for me as I hear the scuttling of something under me. I reach the top and throw my arms out, grabbing onto loose roots from the grass. I try to pull myself up, but the hand from before grabs onto my leg again and pulls me down. I try to hold onto the roots, but they snap from the pressure, and I slip down the shaft, landing on the hard floor once more.

Sharp pain cuts through my spine and skull. I groan as I roll onto my side, feeling the warm ground touch my bare arms. The blood from my nose continues to stream down my chin as my vision distorts the room around me. The walls seem to spin, and the ceiling pulses to the same rhythm as my heart. The sounds of the buzzing flies bounce from ear to ear. I roll onto my stomach as, from the corner of my eye, the shadowy figure crawls from under the bed.

As it walks into the light, the shadow fades from its body. I can see the authentic look of the figure. Looks very human-like, with pale gray skin and a tuft of brown hair atop his large forehead. His eyes sink into his face, his nose curving and covering his lipless, gaping mouth. As for his clothing, he wears none. Scars and deep cuts wrap around his bare skin. The most grotesque detail of all; his throat has a deep slit chapped with dried blood.

It stumbles toward me with a limp; its left knee is twisted toward the right. But, with my vision still warped, it looks like the creature has doubled. Through my disturbed eyes, I can see the figure's arms begin to grow downward, extending inhumanely. As I nauseously use my elbows to stand up, the creature's fingertips reach the ground, making a loud screeching sound as they dig through the concrete.

Once the figure is within reach, I grab onto one of the arms, feeling the cold squishy skin as its head stares at me with its dark, empty eyes. My face turns into a facade of terror as it digs its other arm into my back with its sharp fingernails. My hands let go as the monster lifts me up and throws me into the bedroom. I crash onto the bed, and as I try to roll off, the bed frame makes a loud cracking noise and collapses onto the ground. Damaged parts of the structure fly in the air, with a few falling inches from my exhausted body.

My back feels as though it's not even connected anymore. I can feel the internal bleeding that a ruptured spine most definitely caused.

Let's hope I still have a few medicarrel packs left.

I crack open the front of my corset, revealing a black bra and a scar-covered stomach, while being careful not to let any buttons hit my face. On the inside of it are many hidden pockets, perfect for storage. A bag of medicare needles is among the puny daggers and bullets I have stashed away. Being manufactured by Blood Plus Inc., these needles are perfect for someone like me who gets in a fight every other day. So I toss the broken corset onto the ground, still lying down from the throw, as I search each pocket for a needle.

Bullets…paper? Let's see…this pocket should have some…no… that's a finger. Here it is!

I pull something from one of the pockets, a small, gray tube with a needle on one end and a square button on the other. I jam it into my left arm, that's paler than our moons, and press the button. The liquid inside shoots into my veins, and I feel my body repair itself. The bleeding stops, my spine corrects its position, and the blood from my nose swims back up my nostrils.

The figure walks up to the doorway and stares at my healed body. I stare back through the messy hair that blocks my face. It makes its way toward me again, and I frantically look around the room for a weapon. My eyes dart to the green folding chair, so I jump over and grab onto it.

Once I feel the monster's presence behind me, I turn around, slamming the chair into its face. The chair cracks its jaw, and a few teeth fly out and make a dink sound as they hit the floor. Blood splatters onto the chair and the wall, creating designs akin to the paintings seen in Carishem's Museum of Art. I take another swing, bashing the chair into the creature's open neck wound. Blood squirts onto my face, going into my eyes and causing me to stumble back into the wall.

I keep swinging the chair as I close my eyes to avoid blood getting into my eyes. I feel each impact as the metal chair clanking against its skull echoes through the room. I hold the chair above my head and throw it downward, hearing two impacts. One was most definitely the hit. The other is a victory. I wipe my eyelids and open them to see the monster lying on the ground. Its face and neck are beaten, with blood drooling onto the floor.

The brain and gums are exposed, with teeth bent out of place in the twisted mouth. The skin flaps and pieces of gore cover the eyes to the point that they cannot be seen. The chair lies next to the disturbed corpse, hidden in the blood of the fallen. The green and red mix like an Earth Christmas decoration. I quickly place my hands on my knees and gasp for air.

What just happened? This is not Julia-N; it doesn't match the photo from before.

After I catch my breath, I pick up my corset, step over the body and walk into the middle room. The Zargon corpse continues to be eaten by little bugs that crawl through the walls. I walk into the dark room, trying to light it up again, but when nothing works, I return to the ladder. Before climbing back up, I look up the hole to see the cloudless orange sky. I take a deep breath, then climb up to the surface.

To the West, the sun sets as the many Locanagwan moons rise to the East. I grab a match from my broken corset, light it on the stone pathway under me, and throw it down the hole. Once I can see the glow of orange from the bottom of the void, I close the hatch to the bunker. I wipe sweat from my forehead as I walk off to return to Marz.

—

The path from Carishem to the nightclub is not that far on foot, only about seventeen miles between each. The lounge I get my jobs from is located in the town of Lükahmp. Named after a courageous warrior that fought in the Locanagwan Freedom Fights during 1412 BDL (Before Death of Locanagwo, a famous ruler and dictator of Loca). Lükahmp is a relatively small town, with only a few metal houses and two shops, along with, of course, the nightclub.

The town is mainly populated with scum. Assassins, addicts, and even some of Al-X's close friends. I don't own a house, but I live in an apartment a few blocks from the club. I live on the seventh floor, in room 709. The apartment has only three rooms. The first is a small bedroom that can only fit my single bed. The front room is a small kitchen which is taken up by my fridge, a counter, and two high-hanging shelves. The last is a medium-sized living room, occupied by a dusty brown couch and a window to show the view of the slummy town.

After returning to Marz, collecting my reward of a month of free Klambinoshy fruits, I walk into my apartment and crash onto the living room couch. A breeze runs through the room, brushing against my sensitive stomach. I wheeze with coldness, and so I get off the couch to get a blanket. I walk into my small bedroom, where my neatly made blue bed invites me to sleep.

I crawl under the heavy covers, putting my head in between the two yellow pillows. The bedroom window lets the tiniest amount of moonlight into my room, which doesn't annoy me.

What even was today? I guess I should tell Marz the truth about Julia-N.

My eyelids slowly close as the room around me darkens. I have a loud yawn that immediately puts me to sleep. I have dreams about living on another planet and selling plants. Perhaps on Inaz?

What a remarkable life. Hopefully, one day, though I doubt it.

www.ingramcontent.com/pod-product-compliance
Lightning Source LLC
Chambersburg PA
CBHW032127170626
46808CB00006B/2128